OH!はいㄠ~ Anにょんすかㅔllyo! How알ゆ~

Touch the world,
It's so EZ.

OH!はいら～ AnにょんはMIyo! How알유～

Touch the world,
It's so EZ.

台灣人最容易犯錯的英文問題全收錄
一句生活會話，搞懂10大惱人文法問題

= *Did you know that vodka is made of / **from** potatoes?*
你知道伏特加是用馬鈴薯做的嗎？

# 惱人啊！
# 講N遍你還錯的英文文法

*I'm raised by/**on** junk food.*
我是吃垃圾食物長大的。

*I saw the news on/**in** the newspaper.*
我在報紙上看到那則消息。

*If the weather will be/**is** nice, I may go to the beach.*
如果天氣好的話，我應該會去海邊。

*be sure to pack lightly/**light**.*
記得要帶輕便的行李。

*I don't like stinky tofu neither/**either**.*
我也不喜歡臭豆腐。

*The old needs/**need** more medical care than the young.*
長者比年輕人更需要醫療照護。

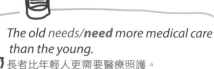

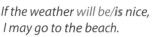

# 目錄
# Contents

## 冠詞 Articles

# Chapter 1
# 介系詞
## *prepositions*

為何介系詞這麼惱人啊！？

介系詞本身沒有意義，英文卻有超過 150 個不同介系詞，幾乎無法只靠字面上意思來幫助記憶。

We are ***at the hospital*** visiting a friend who's ***in the hospital***.
介系詞的搭配，不管是搭名詞、動詞還是形容詞，不一樣的介系詞搭出來的意思完全不同，出糗機率高到破錶！

She met ~~up with~~ her new boss ~~at~~ downstairs.
不知如何適當使用介系詞，要不就不用，要不就用太多，搞得說話和聽話的人一個頭兩個大，頭都暈了。

# 介系詞大哉問
## Questions About Using Prepositions

介系詞這般惱人，反正沒幾個字母，可以乾脆不用它嗎？

人生啊！什麼事情都由你來選，豈不是全都亂了套？

介系詞在英文句子裡就是圈住兩個字詞間關係的線，可以敘述這句話裡到底發生啥事，也可以增加句中的訊息。很抽象嗎？看看以下句子：

I put the keys the doormat.
鑰匙跟門墊，你放了這兩個物品，然後咧？聽不懂！

I put the keys under the doormat.
喔～你把鑰匙放在門墊下啦！哉了，等等我去拿！

再來一句感覺看看，有了介系詞，句子有 fu 多了：

The prince climbed the wall.
嗯，王子爬了牆。是爬得很辛苦？還是站在牆上看啥？沒重點！

The prince climbed over the wall into the witch's garden.
喔～原來王子翻過牆進了巫婆的花園拉！接下來會發生什麼事情呢？真刺激！

懂了吧？句子如果少了介系詞，意思會破碎不通順，而在這個資訊爆炸時代，把想法表達得清楚又通順是何其重要？介系詞絕對能讓你說話切中要點、精彩絕倫！

好啦好啦，我學就是了，但至少告訴我到底有幾種介系詞？

浪子回頭金不換啊！既然你決定不當塊說話無味的木頭了，我就告訴你個好消息！其實介系詞雖超過 150 個不同字，且每個介系詞接了別的字還不一定同意思，看似記不完，但若從介系詞的主要表達來看，就可分出以下幾種基本款：

▶ 地點及位置介系詞：表達一個動作 / 名詞和一個地點的關係
sit <u>on</u> the chair、walk <u>in</u> the park、books <u>on</u> the shelves

▶ 時間介系詞：表達一動作 / 名詞和發生時間的關係
eat dinner <u>in</u> the evening、read <u>on</u> weekends、the movie <u>at</u> 8:00

▶ 行動介系詞：表達一動作 / 名詞的移動狀態
walk <u>through</u> the park、go <u>to</u> the library、a man <u>from</u> the U.S.

▶ 慣用搭配介系詞：常與動詞、形容詞、名詞搭配使用的介系詞，須當成一個字

來記意思：

belong to（屬於）、capable of（有能力）、concerned about（擔心）

聽起來還是很難啊～（跺腳）！？難怪我學這麼久都學不好！

說介系詞不難就是在騙人了，不然我們幹嘛還要教？說了這本是「最容易犯錯」文法，當然有其難度在。不過別擔心，接下來的課程就是要讓你介系詞功力大進，搞懂這些題目，常用的那些介系詞都不怕再表錯情了，剩下的就要靠多閱讀囉！等等，還沒結束，學介系詞還是有些訣竅的：

▶ 介系詞本身不具意義，所以一定要連同前後連接的名詞、動詞等一起記憶，如此才有助於聯想。

▶ 介系詞跟你想表達情境屬「靜態」還是「動態」很有關係，譬如 in、on、at、under……這些就是靜止的，from、to、through、over……這些則是有某種動感的。靜止的介系詞的選擇使用重點是「位置的關係」，動態介系詞重點則是「移動方向／方式」。

「我喜歡在公園裡散步」，你是在說明喜好，就屬於靜態情境：

I like to walk in the park.

「我正在往公園走去」，這時你想說的是進行的方向，要選帶有「往…去」意味的介系詞 to：

I'm walking to the park.

▶ 千萬別呆呆的以為某個詞只能使用某個固定介系詞。從上兩句例子就可知，一切還是取決於你想表達的意思。例如「在床上」說 on the bed 就錯，一定要用 in bed 嗎？學介系詞除了記憶固定用法，還是可按照語意活用搭配的！

{ **我是吃垃圾食物長大的。** }

▶「長大」是用 grow up 這個片語嗎？
▶ be raised 後面常會接 on 或 by，意思差在哪？

🔍 你先選選看

A: What happened to the boy after his parents died?
B: He was raised **by / on** his grandparents.

A: 那個男孩在他父母死後怎麼樣了？
B: 他被祖父母撫養長大。

---

A: Why are you so unhealthy?
B: I was raised **by / on** junk food.

A: 你怎麼這麼不健康？
B: 因為我是吃垃圾食物長大的。

Ans: by, on

---

▶ 表達「長大」的確可用 grow up 這個片語，但是強調「被養育長大」，則要用 be raised。

▶ be raised on 是「以某種方式長大」，而 be raised by 則是「被誰帶大」，語意完全不同，所以用介系詞時不可不慎。

Many children are raised <u>by</u> single parents.
許多孩子是由單親父母撫養。

I was raised <u>on</u> rock, but now I like country.
我是聽搖滾樂長大的，但我現在喜歡鄉村音樂。

Bill was raised <u>on</u> a farm.
比爾是在農村長大的。

▶ 要是搞不清楚，就直接記 by 和 on 這兩個介系詞最根本的差別：

by　被…

| The man was hit <u>by</u> a car while crossing the street.
那名男子過馬路時被車撞到。

on　憑藉／倚靠…

| It's hard to live <u>on</u> such a low wage.
靠這麼少的薪水很難生活。

| The car runs <u>on</u> electricity.
這輛車是以電作動力。

都幫你整理好，不要再問了！
be raised on... 在…的狀況下長大
be raised by... 被…養大

# 你的包裹應該兩星期內會到。

▶ 介系詞 in 和 within 都有「在…之內」的意思,那要表達「在某段時間內」,到底要用哪個介系詞?

## 你先選選看

A: How long will the shipment take?
B: Your package should arrive **in / within** two weeks.

A: 貨要多久才會到?
B: 你的包裹應該兩星期內會到。

---

A: Why are you in such a hurry?
B: I have to be at work **in / within** 15 minutes.

A: 你幹嘛這麼急?
B: 我十五分鐘後要到公司。

Ans: within, in

▶ 要表達「在某段時間內」要用 within,例如:

I'll be back within three days.
我三天內會回來。
→ 一天後、兩天後或是第三天回來都有可能

▶ 而用 in,則表示「在某時間點之後」,例如:

I'll be back in three days.
我三天後會回來。
→ 起碼要過三天才會回來

多學一點，加深印象！

▷ 在時間的表達上，表示「在…之內」的介系詞還有 during，但是跟 within 不同的是，during 比較強調「整段時間」都在進行該動作，較有延續性，例如：

The museum is closed during the month of August.
博物館整個八月都在休館。

▷ within 通常是用在「某段時間中的一個時間點」：

An announcement will be made within the next 24 hours.
接下來二十四小時內會作一項宣布。

都幫你整理好，不要再問了！
within + 時間→在某段時間內
in + 時間→過了（某時間）之後

across
out of
opposite
under
front
on
between
over

# 你知道伏特加是用馬鈴薯做的嗎？

▶ 我知道「某物是…做的」，動詞要用 make 的被動形態 be made，但是後面介系詞到底是接 from 還是 of，要怎麼判斷呢？

## 🔍 你先選選看

A: Did you know that vodka is made **from / of** potatoes?
B: I had no idea.

A: 你知道伏特加是用馬鈴薯做的嗎？
B: 我不知道耶。

---

A: Why is this shirt so comfortable?
B: It's made **from / of** cotton.

A: 這件襯衫怎麼穿起來那麼舒服？
B: 因為它是棉製的。

Ans: from, of

---

▶ 要用 be made of 或 be made from，主要是看該物的「性質」有無改變，例如伏特加的外觀、質感，甚至是味道，都跟它的原料「馬鈴薯」差很多，根本看不出來兩者關聯，這時就要用 be made from；而當可以察覺該物的原料時，則要用 be made of：

Cheese is made <u>from</u> milk.
起司是用牛奶做的。

Paper is made <u>from</u> wood.
紙是用木材做的。

The building is made of bricks.
這棟建築是用磚頭蓋成的。

These earrings are made of silver.
這對耳環是銀製的。

多學一點，加深印象！

▶ 除了 be made of 和 be made from，我們還常聽到 made in + 地名，表示某物是「在哪裡製造的」。

Most of the cameras we sell are made in Japan.
我們所賣的相機大部份都是日本製的。

across

out of

opposite

under

front

on

between

over

# 我看報紙上寫的。

▷ 那天想講在報紙上看到某則新聞，突然不知該用 in the newspaper 還是 on the newspaper，感覺好像兩者都說得通，到底該用哪個呢？

## 你先選選看

A: How do you know that star is getting married?
B: I read it **in / on** the newspaper.

A: 你怎麼知道那個明星要結婚了？
B: 我看報紙上寫的。

---

A: Why isn't Allen at work?
B: He's **in / on** bed with a flu.

A: 艾倫怎麼沒上班？
B: 他得了流感臥病在床。

Ans: in, in

▷ in 和 on 雖然很容易辨別，但是拿來描述比較抽象的意義時，卻很容易搞混。雖然中文會說：「我在報紙上看到一則新聞。」，但是英文 on the newspaper 是指有東西放在報紙上，in the newspaper 才是指報紙寫的內容，其他的讀物像雜誌、書籍等的用法也是一樣。

There are many interesting characters in the book.
這本書裡有許多有趣的角色。

His article appeared in a news magazine.
他的文章被登在新聞雜誌上。

▶ in bed 通常是指「蓋著被子躺在床上」；on the bed 則是單純指「在床的上面」。

The cat is sleeping <u>on the bed</u>.
那隻貓睡在床上。

都幫你整理好，不要再問了！
記越多只會越混淆，只要記清楚常用用法就行了：
<u>in</u> the newspaper　在報紙上（指刊登的文章、圖片等）
<u>in</u> bed　（躺）在床上

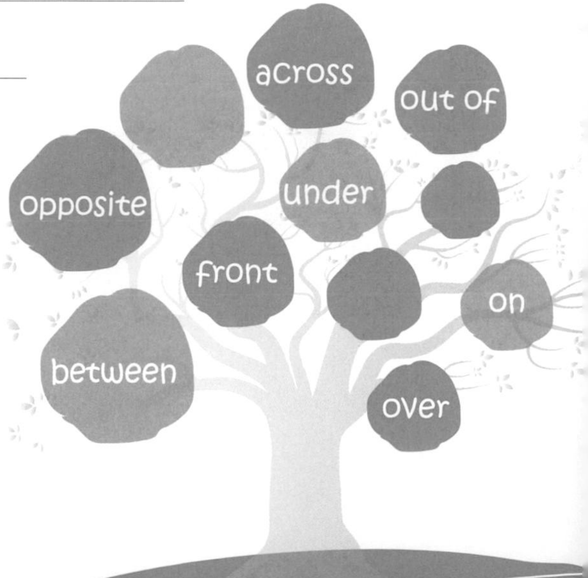

across

out of

opposite

under

front

on

between

over

# 可以請你吃飯時不要抽菸嗎？

▶ 想表達「用餐」，要說 at the table 還是 on the table?

## 🔍 你先選選看

A: Would you mind not smoking **at / on** the table?
B: Sorry. I'll put it out.

A: 可以請你吃飯時不要抽菸嗎？
B: 不好意思。我會把它熄掉。

---

A: Have you seen my keys?
B: I think you left them **at / on** the table.

A: 你有看到我的鑰匙嗎？
B: 你大概放在桌上吧。

Ans: at, on

▶ at 是「在（某處）」的意思，而 on 則解釋為「在…之上」。at the table 指的是「面對著餐／桌子」，on the table 則是「在桌子上面」。中文裡，當我們說在餐桌「上」用餐，可不是真的站在桌子上面，所以英文要用 at the table，而不是 on the table。

> Don't talk on your cell phone when you're <u>at the table</u>.
> 在餐桌上吃飯時不要講手機。

多學一點，加深印象！

> on the table 可以單純指東西放在「桌子上」，也可用來指某項計劃或建議正
> 在考慮或洽談。

The proposal is still <u>on the table</u>.
這項提案還在討論當中。

A: I thought the player said he wasn't considering switching teams.
B: Yes, but now there's a new offer <u>on the table</u>.

A: 我以為那名球員說他沒有考慮換到別隊。
B: 對啊，不過現在有個新機會正在談。

都幫你整理好，不要再問了！
at the table　吃飯時
on the table　在桌上；（計畫、建議）提交考慮

# 有人打電話來找我嗎？

▶ 「打電話」不是直接用 call + 人就好了嗎？為什麼有時 call 後面會加 for ？

🔍 你先選選看

A: Did anyone **call / call for** me while I was out.
B: Yeah. Kelly called about an hour ago.

A: 我外出的時候有人打來找我嗎？
B: 有。凱莉大概一個小時前有打來。

Ans: call for

▶ call / phone「打電話」後面要直接加上受詞（人或地點），不過，在口語上若 call 後面接 for，則有 call（asking）for sb.「打電話找某人」的意味。

Maria called the fire department immediately when she saw the burning house.
瑪麗亞一看到房子失火，立刻打電話給消防隊。

Your dad called for you while you were out.
你出去時你爸有打電話來找你。

 都幫你整理好，不要再問了！
call + 人 / 地點　打電話給⋯
call for + 人　打電話找⋯

{ **跟休比起來，你簡直就是喬治克隆尼。** }

▶ 拿 A 和 B 相比，動詞片語是要用 compare to 還是 compare with ？

🔍 你先選選看

A: I don't think I'm very handsome.
B: Maybe not. But compared **to / with** Hugh, you're George Clooney.

A: 我覺得我沒有很帥。
B: 或許吧。但跟休比起來，你簡直就是喬治克隆尼了。

> Ans: to

▶ compare 有兩種解釋，一為「比較，對照」，另一個則是「比喻為…，比作…」。

▶ compare to 通常可用來界定相同或不同處，或是用來作比喻；compare with 則是同時比較異同，但口語中則沒分得那麼嚴謹，有時可互相替換使用。

The critic compared Duke Ellington's music <u>to</u> the music of Beethoven.
樂評把威靈頓公爵的音樂和貝多芬相比。

The poet compared his lover's smile <u>to</u> the sun.
那首詩將愛人的笑容比作太陽。

The teacher asked me to compare the American government <u>with</u> the British government.
老師要我把美國政府和英國政府作番比較。

💬 都幫你整理好，不要再問了！
compare A to B　比較；將 A 比喻成 B
compare A with B　比較 A 和 B

# 我想學英語以外的另一種語言。

▶ besides 和 beside 我老是搞不清楚，請問兩者意思和用法有何不同？

## 你先選選看

A: Do you play any other sports **beside / besides** baseball?
B: Yeah. I also play soccer.

A: 你除了打棒球外，還有沒有做其他運動？
B: 有。我還會踢足球。

Ans: besides

▶ beside 是「在…旁邊」之意，用來敘述位置，而 besides 則是「除了…之外；另外」之意。

The inn is <u>beside</u> a small lake.
那間小旅館在一座小湖邊。

<u>Besides</u> being a classmate, he's also my friend.
他除了是我的同學，也是我的朋友。

I want to learn other languages <u>besides</u> English.
我除了英文，還想學其他語言。

▶ besides 還有「而且，再說」的意思

We don't need a new car. <u>Besides</u>, we can't even afford one.
我們不需要一台新車。再說我們根本就買不起。

多學一點，加深印象！

▶要表示「除了…之外；另外」，更正式的說法為 in addition to：

In addition to French, he also speaks Spanish.
除了法文，他也會講西班牙文。

across

out of

opposite

under

front

on

between

over

都幫你整理好，不要再問了！
beside　在…旁邊
besides　除了…之外；另外

# 買禮物給什麼都不缺的人還真難。

▶ 表達「缺乏」是用 lack 這個字，什麼時候要用 a lack of，什麼時候不用加 a ？

🔍 你先選選看

A: Why are they building a new parking garage?
B: There's **lack / a lack** of parking spaces downtown.

A: 為什麼他們要蓋一間新的停車場？
B: 因為市中心缺少停車位。

---

A: Why didn't Steve ask the girl out?
B: Because he **lacks / a lack** confidence

A: 史蒂夫怎麼沒邀那個女孩出來約會？
B: 因為他缺乏自信。

Ans: a lack, lacks

▶ lack 可當名詞或動詞用，當名詞時，後方才會出現介系詞 of，通常會以單數或不可數形式出現。

▶ lack of + N 和 a lack of + N，差別在於前者指的是「匱乏」的這個抽象狀態，而加了冠詞 a，則是指「某種（特定的）匱乏」。

Rural districts are suffering from a lack of qualified teachers.
鄉下學區苦於缺乏合格教師。

Poor diet and lack of exercise can lead to high blood pressure.
飲食不良加上缺乏運動會導致高血壓。

多學一點，加深印象！

▶ lack 當動詞時，後方可以直接加上缺乏物：

It's hard to buy a gift for someone who <u>lacks</u> nothing.
要買禮物給什麼都不缺的人還真難。

across

out of

opposite

under

front

on

between

over

💬 都幫你整理好，不要再問了！

**a lack of + N**

lack 在此是一個單數名詞「缺乏」，a lack of 則指「某種（特定的）匱乏」。

**lack of + N**

lack 在此是不可數名詞，指「缺乏的狀態」。

# 我喜歡各式各樣的運動。

▶ 介系詞 into 是「進入」的意思，但與人對話時常聽到「be into + 一件事物」這樣的句型，請問是什麼意思呢？

## 你先選選看

A: What kinds of sports do you like?
B: I'm **into / within** all kinds of sports.

A: 你喜歡哪種運動？
B: 我喜歡各式各樣的運動。

Ans: into

▶ be into + 受詞是一個固定片語，表「喜歡」的意思，是相當口語的說法，在電影中、一般對話裡都常常會聽到，後面也常接 just 和 really 來加強語氣。

What kind of music are you into?
你喜歡什麼音樂？

I'm really into Japanese manga.
我超愛日本漫畫。

That guy over there is totally into you.
那邊那個男的很哈妳喔。

多學一點，加深印象！

▶ be into 意同於 like，但除了「喜歡」外，更有「熱衷、投入」的意味，程度較為強烈。

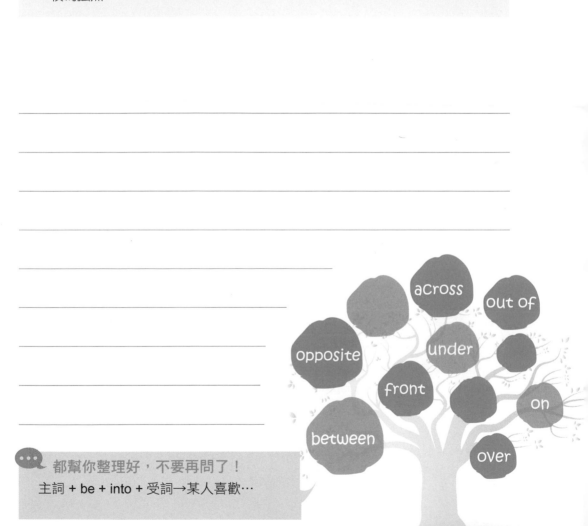

都幫你整理好，不要再問了！
主詞 + be + into + 受詞→某人喜歡…

{ 比賽因天候不佳取消了。 }

▶ because 什麼時候會接介系詞 of？

A: Why didn't you call me?
B: **Because of / Because** I lost your number.

A: 你為什麼沒打給我？
B: 因為我把你號碼弄丟了。

---

A: There was no game yesterday?
B: No. It was cancelled **because of / because** bad weather.

A: 昨天沒球賽嗎？
B: 沒有。球賽因為天候不佳取消了。

Ans: Because, because of

▶ because 是連接詞，用來連接兩個句子，表示「因為」，可替換為 because of 的說法，但後面必須接名詞或動名詞：

Because the weather was cold, we stayed home.
= Because of the cold weather, we stayed home.
因為天氣冷，所以我們待在家裡。

Carey was late to the meeting because the traffic was heavy.
= Carey was late to the meeting because of the heavy traffic.
凱莉因為塞車而開會遲到。

多學一點，加深印象！

▶ because of 還可代換成 due to，後面一樣都接名詞或動名詞，而非完整的句子：

Because of an engine failure, the plane made an emergency landing.
= Due to an engine failure, the plane made an emergency landing.
= Because an engine failed, the plane made an emergency landing.
由於引擎故障，所以那架飛機緊急迫降。

都幫你整理好，不要再問了！
because + 主詞＋動詞
because of + 名詞／動名詞

# 我分不出紅色和綠色。

▶ tell 當「分辨」時，後面接 by 或 from 的差別在哪？

## 你先選選看

A: How do you know that guy is rich?
B: You can tell **by / from** the car he drives.

A: 你怎麼知道那男的很有錢？
B: 看他開的車就知道了。

---

A: I can't tell red **by / from** green.
B: You must be color blind.

A: 我分不出紅色和綠色。
B: 你一定是色盲。

Ans: by, from

▶ tell 這個動詞常常做「分辨；確定」使用，在英文中常聽到 It's hard to tell. 也就是說「很難說、說不準」的意思。

▶ 若想進一步說明做決定的「根據」，tell 之後會接 by 這個介系詞，by 後面接的是「判別的依據」；tell 後面出現另一個介系詞 from 時，解釋為「辨別、識別」。

Can you <u>tell</u> who that is over there?
你看得出來那邊那個人是誰嗎？

I could tell <u>by</u> the depressed look on his face that Jane rejected his proposal.
從他那沮喪的神情看來，我可以確定珍拒絕了他的求婚。

The twin brothers look so much alike that I have trouble telling one <u>from</u> the other.
這對雙胞胎兄弟如此相似，以致於我分辨不出他們誰是誰。

多學一點，加深印象！

▶ tell 當「分辨」之意時，搭配的介系詞還有 apart。tell...apart 就是「分辨出…」。

The twins are so similar that only their parents can <u>tell</u> them <u>apart</u>.
那對雙胞胎像到只有爸媽才分得出他們誰是誰。

Can you <u>tell</u> Chinese people <u>apart</u> from Japanese people?
你能分得出來中國人和日本人嗎？

都幫你整理好，不要再問了！
tell（A）by（B）　從（A）而確定（B）
tell A from B　分辨出 A 與 B

# { 我住在街角那棟房子。 }

▶ 「在角落」要用 in the corner 還是 on the corner？

## 🔍 你先選選看

A: Where do you live?
B: I live in that house **in / on** the corner.

A: 你住在哪裡？
B: 我住在街角那棟房子。

---

A: Why is Mark sitting **in / on** the corner?
B: He's being punished for talking in class.

A: 為何馬克坐在角落？
B: 他因為上課講話被處罰。

Ans: on, in

▶ corner 是「轉角」的意思，但如果用的介系詞不同，意思也就不同。

▶ on the corner 可用在街角，或是像書桌一角，這種開放空間的角落；in the corner 用來指稱室內或內部的轉角，比如屋子裡的一角：

There's a gas station on the corner.
街角有間加油站。

Will this cabinet fit in the corner?
這個櫃子放得進這個角落嗎？

💬 都幫你整理好，不要再問了！
on the corner　街角；轉角的上方
in the corner　在室內或內部的角落

# 他看起來好面熟。

▶ familiar 後面何時要接 with，何時要接 to?

 你先選選看

A: I think that guy used to live in our building.
B: No wonder he looks so familiar **with / to** me.

A: 那個人好像以前住在我們這棟。
B: 難怪我看他那麼面熟。

---

A: Are you familiar **with / to** this software?
B: Yes. I can show you how to use it.

A: 你對這軟體熟嗎?
B: 熟。我可以教你怎麼用。

Ans: to, with

▶ familiar to 和 familiar with 都有「對…很熟悉」的意思，但用法上有些差異，
familiar to + 人，表示某事物讓某人感到熟悉；人 + be familiar with + 事物，則是
表示某人對某事很熟悉。

This song sounds familiar to me.
這首歌我聽起來覺得很熟悉。

Are you familiar with this song?
你知道這首歌嗎？

💬 都幫你整理好，不要再問了！

...be familiar to sb.　某事讓某人感到熟悉

S + be familiar with...　某人知道…，某人對…很熟悉

# 你有準時上班嗎？

▶ 「準時」是 in time 還是 on time ？

🔍 你先選選看

A: Did you get there **in / on** time to see your wife give birth?
B: No. Unfortunately, I missed it.

A: 你有及時趕上看到你太太生產嗎？
B: 沒有。很可惜，我錯過了。

---

A: Did you get to work **in / on** time?
B: No. I was five minutes late.

A: 你有準時上班嗎？
B: 沒有。我晚了五分鐘。

Ans: in, on

▶ 當 time 前面的介系詞是 in 時，表「及時」，也就是來得及做某事的意思。

The fire engine didn't arrive <u>in time</u> to save the burning building.
消防車沒有及時趕到現場拯救那棟失火的大樓。

▶ 但如果將介系詞換成 on 時，意思是「準時」，也就是按照原訂時間，沒有遲到。

In Switzerland, the trains always arrive <u>on time</u>.
在瑞士，火車總是準點。

 都幫你整理好，不要再問了！
on time　準時
in time　及時

## { 那間餐廳在銀行和郵局之間。 }

▶ between 和 among 都有「在…之間」的意思，用法有什麼差別嗎？

🔍 你先選選看

A: Where is the restaurant?
B: It's **between / among** the bank and the post office.

A: 那間餐廳在哪裡？
B: 在銀行和郵局之間。

---

A: How did he learn the tribe's language?
B: He lived **between / among** them for years.

A: 他怎麼學會那個部落的語言？
B: 他跟他們一起生活了好幾年。

Ans: between, among

▶ between 是指「兩者之間」，例如，between you and me（我和你之間）、between Jack and Sue（傑克與蘇之間）；among 則是用在「三者以上」，例如 among the books（書堆中）、 among the crowd（人群中）。

The boy sat <u>between</u> his parents.
那個男孩坐在他爸媽之間。

There's a small cabin hidden <u>among</u> the trees.
樹叢間有一間小屋。

 都幫你整理好，不要再問了！
between 兩者之間
among 「三者以上／一群…之間」

# { 說到帥，你有看過蜜雅的新男友嗎？ }

▶ 口語對話常會出現「說到…」，英文要怎麼說？

## 你先選選看

A: That guy over there is so hot.
B: Speaking **of / for** hot, have you seen Mia's new boyfriend?

A: 那邊那個男的好帥。
B: 說到帥，妳有看過蜜雅的新男友嗎？

---

A: That candidate claims to speak **of / for** most young voters.
B: I seriously doubt that.

A: 那位候選人聲稱會幫年輕選民發聲。
B: 我實在很懷疑。

Ans: of, for

▶ speak of 和 speak for 常讓人混淆，speak of 是「提及」之意，而 speaking of 則是一個固定用法，通常是在說話時提到某件事，進而想起這件事情的相關事物，就會用這個片語開啟另一個話題。

Speaking of Italian food, have you tried that new Italian place downtown?
說到義大利菜，你去吃過市中心那間新的義大利餐廳了嗎？

▶ speak for... 即「代表…發言」，在各種公開場合（例如記者會、頒獎典禮等等）都很常見。

They chose Mary to speak for the group.
該團體選瑪麗替他們發言。

▶ 另一個片語 speak for yourself 則是一種慣有說法，指的是「那只代表你自己的意見（不能代表其他人）」。

A: We're too full for dessert.
　　我們太飽了，吃不下甜點。

B: Speak for yourself. I'd like a slice of pie.
　　那是你喔。我還想吃一塊派。

都幫你整理好，不要再問了！

speak of...　提及⋯

speak for...　代表⋯發言

# 你什麼時候會到臺北？

▶ 每次要描述「到達某地點」，用 in、on 還是 at 老是搞不清楚，到底要怎麼選用呢？

🔍 你先選選看

A: When will you arrive **in / at** Taipei?
B: Next Wednesday.

A: 你什麼時候會到臺北？
B: 下星期三。

---

A: Did the police catch the robbers?
B: No. When they arrived **in / at** the bank, the robbers were already gone.

A: 警察有抓到那票搶匪嗎？
B: 沒有。他們到銀行的時候，搶匪已經跑了。

---

A: Your office threw you a surprise party?
B: Yeah. When I arrived **in / on** our floor, everyone was waiting outside the elevator.

A: 你公司有幫你辦驚喜派對喔？
B: 對啊。我到我們那層樓的時候，大家都在電梯外等我。

Ans: in, at, on

▶ 動詞 arrive 之後搭配的介系詞，要依據地方的規模來選擇，如果是範圍較大，例如城市或國家，就用 in；抵達某棟建築物、或是到某場合，用 at；到達某樓層，則用 on。

I just arrived in Brazil yesterday.
我昨天剛到巴西。

We arrived <u>at</u> the airport two hours before our flight.
我們在班機起飛前兩小時到了機場。

When firefighters arrived <u>on</u> the 5th floor, it was too late to put out the fire.
當消防員到五樓的時候，要撲滅這場火已經太遲了。

💬 都幫你整理好，不要再問了！
arrive in ＋ 城市、國家
arrive at ＋ 建築物、場合
arrive on ＋ 樓層

across
out of
opposite
under
front
on
between
over

# 介系詞總複習
請選出適當的答案

1. The cattle are raised _____ a diet of grain and hay.
    A. by
    B. on
    C. from
    D. of

2. Wine is made _____ grapes.
    A. by
    B. on
    C. from
    D. of

3. Who else knows about this _____ you?
    A. besides
    B. other
    C. beside
    D. except

4. Is there anything _____ the paper about the plane crash?
    A. among
    B. on
    C. within
    D. in

5. The restaurant closed due to _____ customers.
    A. lack of
    B. a lack of
    C. lack
    D. a lack

6. Some people think it's rude to wear a hat _____ the table.

    A. off

    B. on

    C. in

    D. at

7. The post office is _____ the corner.

    A. on

    B. in

    C. at

    D. up

8. I'm not really _____ electronic music.

    A. in

    B. into

    C. in to

    D. onto

9. He was hired _____ his computer experience.

    A. because

    B. since

    C. because of

    D. due

10. I can never tell her _____ her sister.

    A. from

    B. to

    C. by

    D. as

解答

1. B  2. C  3. A  4. D  5. B

6. D  7. A  8. B  9. C  10. A

# *Chapter 2*
# 形容詞 & 副詞
## Adjectives and Adverbs

副詞和形容詞的惱人之處：

種類繁多，規則、不規則變化一堆，有些副詞和形容詞根本是同一個字，讓人常常錯亂，一個頭兩個大。

有些形容詞字尾加 ly 即可成為副詞，但有些加 ly 後意思卻不相同，容易用錯，例如 late（晚的，遲的）和 lately（最近）。

**That scary movie makes me scared.**
形容的對象是「人」或「事物」，形容詞會有不同的變化，不能一個形容詞用到底。

# 形容詞 & 副詞大哉問
## Questions About Using Adjectives and Adverbs

最基本的直述句就是 S（主詞）+ V（動詞）+ O（受詞），形容詞和副詞好像不是必需的，不用有差嗎？

拜託，想展現英文實力，只會講這麼陽春的句型 OK 嗎？千萬不要小看這些用來修飾句子的小幫手，想要詢問或描述事物，沒有形容詞和副詞怎麼成得了事？你看：

I went to a movie last night.
我昨晚去看了一場電影。

喔，你昨晚看了一場電影。那是什麼電影啊？恐怖片？喜劇片？浪漫愛情片？

I watched a romantic movie last night.
我昨晚看了一場浪漫愛情電影。

是喔，你看的是浪漫愛情片。你覺得如何？好看嗎？

The movie is very touching and inspiring.
那部電影既感人又鼓舞人心。

既然你都這麼說了，那我也去看看吧！

有沒有發現，這段對話要是少了形容詞，根本第一句講完就卡住了吧！完全沒辦法提供額外的資訊，聊不下去。同理，副詞也是一樣重要，不僅可以提升句子豐富度，還能補充許多資訊，完整表達當中細節，所以當然要好好學它們的用法囉！

形容詞和副詞有什麼關係，為什麼要放在一起學？

形容詞和副詞可說是哥倆好，都是來給句子「加油添醋」的，不過它們的任務不太一樣，看英文就知道，形容詞的英文是 adjective，objective 本身有「物品、物件」的意思，所以形容詞想當然爾就是用來形容一樣「東西」，也就是名詞啦！而副詞的英文是 adverb，因此它的作用就是修飾動詞（verb），也可修飾形容詞，而許多副詞其實是由形容詞變化而來的，例如：

▶ 形容詞→副詞
careful → carefully
easy → easily
polite → politely

看到上面的例子，聰明的你應該也發現了，很多副詞都是形容詞加 ly 變化而成的，但要是所有字都這麼規律，學英語還會那麼惱人嗎？當然是有很多例外啦，例如以下這些：

▶ 形容詞→副詞
fast → fast
hard → hard
good → well

這些不規則的變化，也只能多看、多背啦！但總之形容詞和副詞的關係是密不可分的，要記就要一起記。

副詞的種類實在是多到不行，擺放的位置也不一定，要怎麼背啊？

要是跟你說…其實這些都不用特別去背，你會覺得聽起來很不「專業」嗎？但事實上，就如本書一再強調的，其實很多文法你不是完全不會，而是有一些令人糾結的小細節讓你不知該如何選擇。一般形容詞和副詞的用法其實多看、多聽句子就自然而然知道該怎麼用了。基本上，副詞大概有這些：

▶ 情狀副詞，說明動作如何發生
He plays basketball <u>well</u>.

▶ 地方副詞，說明動作發生的地點
<u>Here</u> comes the bus.

▶ 時間副詞，說明動作發生的時間
Sam popped the question <u>at last</u>.

▶ 頻率副詞，說明動作多久發生一次
She <u>always</u> brushes her teeth before breakfast.

▶ 程度副詞，說明動作在怎樣的狀況下發生
You are <u>definitely</u> right.

與其背副詞種類，倒不如記一些像上述一樣簡短明確的例子，要用的時候就自然而然就會把副詞放在正確的位置上啦！

## 她沒有以前那麼胖了。

▶ no 和 not 都是用來表示「否定」的意思，用法上有什麼差別？

🔍 你先選選看

A: Is Rebecca still fat?
B: She's **no / not** as fat as she used to be.

A: 蘿貝卡還是很胖嗎？
B: 她沒有以前那麼胖了。

---

A: I said **no / not** fighting in the house!
B: But Dad, he started it!

A: 我說了不准在家裡打架！
B: 爸，可是是他先開始的！

Ans: not, no

▶ not 一定要跟著 be 動詞或助動詞表示否定，或放在名詞前表示「不是…」；no 的後面接名詞時表示「沒有…」，接動名詞（Ving）則表示「禁止／不准…」。

I'm <u>not</u> interested in politics.
我對政治沒興趣。

There's <u>no</u> smoking in the hospital.
醫院裡禁止抽菸。

 都幫你整理好，不要再問了！
no + 名詞／動名詞
be 動詞／助動詞 + not + 形容詞

# { 來派對的人比預期的少。 }

▶ less 和 fewer 都是「較少」的意思，用法上有何區別？

🔍 你先選選看

A: Do you make more money than your brother?
B: No. I make **less / fewer**.

A: 你錢賺得比你弟多嗎？
B: 不。我賺得比較少。

A: Why did that bookstore close?
B: Because people are buying **less / fewer** books these days.

A: 為什麼那家書店關門了？
B: 因為近來人們比較少買書了。

Ans: less, fewer

▶ less 和 fewer 都是「較少」的意思，差別在於後面所接的名詞可不可數。 less 是 little 的比較級，用於不可數名詞；fewer 是 few 的比較級，用於可數名詞。

| You should put <u>less</u> salt on your food.
| 你的食物應該少放點鹽。

| <u>Fewer</u> people came to the party than expected.
| 來派對的人比預期的少。

 都幫你整理好，不要再問了！
less + 不可數名詞
fewer + 可數名詞

# 你喜歡看恐怖片嗎？

▶ 形容詞「嚇人的」，英文是一律都用 scary 嗎？

## 你先選選看

A: Do you like watching **scary / scared** movies?
B: No. They give me nightmares.

A: 你喜歡看恐怖片嗎？
B: 不喜歡。它們會害我做惡夢。

---

A: What are you afraid of?
B: I'm **scary / scared** of spiders.

A: 你怕什麼？
B: 我怕蜘蛛。

Ans: scary, scared

▶ scary 與 scared 兩個字都是形容詞，都有「害怕的」的意思。不過，前者是表示「使人害怕的」，主詞通常具有引起恐懼的本質，例如：蛇、毛蟲、不明原因疾病等。

▶ scared 則和 afraid 一樣，描繪「（人）感到害怕的」的心理狀態，主詞通常為具有情緒起伏的人或動物。兩個字的用法略有不同。scary 可以直接修飾名詞，scared 則必須加上 of 後，才能修飾名詞：

We sat around the fire telling scary stories.
我們圍著營火說鬼故事。

I've always been scared of snakes.
我一直很怕蛇。

多學一點，加深印象！

▶ 從上面的解說，我們知道 scary 主要是形容「事物特質令人害怕」，而 scared 則是形容「人的感受」。概念類似的形容詞還有：

bored / boring

surprised / surprising

frightened / frightening

shocked / shocking

annoyed / annoying

excited / exciting

amazed / amazing

confused / confusing

disappointed / disappointing

tired / tiring

I'm bored with all the boring shows on TV.
我對電視上那些無聊的節目感到無趣。

The amazing magic trick left the audience amazed.
那個驚人的魔術戲法令觀眾嘖嘖稱奇。

都幫你整理好，不要再問了！
scary 令人感到害怕的
scared（人）感到害怕的

# 那位教授的演講好無聊。

▶ so 和 too 都可接形容詞，表示「非常、太」的意思，用法上有何差別？

🔍 你先選選看

A: The professor's lecture was **so / too** boring.
B: Yeah. I almost fell asleep.

A: 那位教授的演講好無聊。
B: 對啊。我都快要睡著了。

---

A: That music is **so / too** loud.
B: Sorry. I'll turn it down.

A: 那音樂太吵了。
B: 抱歉。我關小聲一點。

Ans: so, too

▶ so 跟 too 都可用來修飾形容詞，在中文裡均表示「非常…」、「太…」的意思。不過，兩者用法其實有些不同。

▶ 一般而言，so 比較近似於中文的「非常」，用來表示說話者心中的驚嘆程度；too 則用來強調「超過原本該有的程度」，通常用於負面的形容詞，如 too bad、too low、too ugly 等。

This down jacket is so cheap.
這件羽絨外套真便宜。
→ 買的人覺得買到賺到！

This down jacket is too cheap.
這件羽絨外套也太便宜了吧。
→ 買的人覺得有問題，懷疑是黑心貨！

 都幫你整理好，不要再問了！

so　非常

too　過於…，太

{ **我春假去露營三天。**

▶ 想表達「有…數量的」，該怎麼將數量轉化為形容詞？ }

🔍 你先選選看

A: Did you go anywhere during spring break?
B: Yes. I went on a **three-day / three days** camping trip.

A: 你春假有去哪裡嗎？
B: 有啊。我有去露營三天。

Ans: three-day

數詞＋表示度量衡或單位的名詞＝形容詞

▶ 此時，表示度量衡或單位的名詞應為單數，中間要加上連字號，且單位名詞不加 s。

**a five-day trip**　五天行程的旅行
**a 10-dollar pen**　一支十塊錢的筆

My pickup truck has a 15-gallon gas tank.
我的小貨卡有十五加侖的油箱。

# 那家餐廳的食物很糟。

▶ 表達「很」、「非常」的形容詞 really 和 very，用法上的差別為何？

## 你先選選看

A: Did you read that book I gave you?
B: Yes. I **really / very** enjoyed it.

A: 你有看我給你的那本書嗎？
B: 有啊。我很喜歡。

---

A: Was the test hard?
B: No. It was **really / very** easy.

A: 考試難嗎？
B: 不會。相當簡單。

Ans: really, really / very

▶ 大家常看到 really 就把它當形容詞翻譯成「真的」，但其實口語上 really 和 very 兩個字都是「很」、「非常」的意思，文法上都屬於副詞，但 really 可以修飾形容詞和動詞，very 則只能修飾形容詞。

▶ 「麥克傑克森非常有才華」，英文可以說：

Michael Jackson is <u>very</u> talented.

Michael Jackson is <u>really</u> talented.
（very 和 really 皆可修飾形容詞 talented）

▶「珊卓很喜歡手工藝品」，英文要說：

Sandra <u>really</u> likes handicrafts. （really 修飾動詞 like）

Sandra likes handicrafts <u>very</u> much. （very 修飾形容詞 much，不能說成 Sandra very likes handicrafts. ）

▶ 雖然 very 是用來修飾形容詞的，但當形容詞本就帶有強調、誇大意味時，例如 excellent（意同 very good）、huge（意同 very big）、terrible（意同 very bad）等，就不能用 very 而只能用 really 了。

The food at that restaurant is <u>really</u> awful.
那家餐廳的菜很難吃。

都幫你整理好，不要再問了！
really →修飾形容詞和動詞
very →修飾形容詞

# 這是有史以來最爛的電影！

▶ 很多文法書上都寫 ever 會用在否定句和疑問句，有例外嗎？

▶ 副詞 even 要怎麼用？

## 🔍 你先選選看

A: That movie was terrible.
B: Yeah. It was the worst movie **ever / even**!

A: 那部電影很難看。
B: 對啊。它是有史以來最爛的電影！

---

A: The last mayor was awful.
B: Maybe, but the new one is **ever / even** worse.

A: 上一任市長很糟。
B: 或許吧，但新任市長更是有過之而無不及。

Ans: ever, even

▶ 大家以為 ever 不能於肯定句中出現，但你會發現，實際上例外的狀況很多。像是對話的這一句 the worst movie ever（有史以來最爛的電影）就是 ever 搭配最高級的用法。

│ This was my best birthday ever!
│ 這是我有生以來最棒的生日了！

▶ 除了搭配最高級之外，ever 在肯定句中也常在表示未來條件的 if 子句中出現。

│ If you're ever in town, just give me a call.
│ 要是你進城來，就打個電話給我。

▶ even 則是「連，甚至更⋯」的意思。常常是之前已經提及一件事情後，你要再表達一個程度更強的事情。

Kevin is fat, but his wife is <u>even</u> fatter.
凱文很胖，但他太太甚至比他更胖。

The animated movie was so bad that <u>even</u> kids thought it was boring.
那部動畫電影爛到連小孩都嫌無聊。

都幫你整理好，不要再問了！
ever →搭配最高級，表強調「有史以來最⋯」
even →表「連，甚至更⋯」

# 你最近有看到榮恩嗎？

▶ late 可以當副詞，那和 lately 的意思有何不同？

A: What happens if I return the book **late / lately**?
B: You'll have to pay a fine.

A: 我的書如果逾期還會怎麼樣？
B: 那你就得付罰款。

---

A: Have you seen Ron **late / lately**?
B: Yeah. I had lunch with him last week.

A: 你最近有看到榮恩嘛？
B: 有啊。我上星期才和他一起吃午餐。

Ans: late, lately

▶ late 和 lately 都可當副詞，但意義不同。形容詞 late 表「晚的，遲到的」，因為字尾沒有 -ly，故它常被誤認只有形容詞的用法，其實它可當副詞，表「晚地，遲到地」；lately 則表「最近；不久前」。

We arrived late to the movie and missed the beginning.
我們看電影遲到，沒看到開頭。

I haven't had any time to exercise lately.
我最近都沒時間運動。

 都幫你整理好，不要再問了！
late   晚地，遲到地
lately   最近地，不久前

# { 我的哥哥一個是醫生，一個是律師。 }

▶ the other 和 another 怎麼分？

🔍 你先選選看

A: Do you have **the other / another** pencil I can use?
B: No. But I have a pen.

A: 你有沒有別的鉛筆可以給我用？
B: 沒有。但我有原子筆。

A: What do your two brothers do?
B: One is a doctor, and **the other / another** is a lawyer.

A: 你的兩個哥哥是做什麼的？
B: 一個是醫生，另一個是律師。

Ans: another, the other

▶ the other 與 another 都可當形容詞或代名詞。差異在於 the other 通常是指兩件或成雙的事物，可以譯為「另一個」；another 沒有特別指明「特定人或物」，可譯為「別的，其他的」。

John took off one boot, and then the other.
約翰脫掉一隻靴子，接著脫另一隻。

Mindy ate one piece of pizza, and then another. Soon, there was nothing left in the box.
明蒂吃了一片披薩，接著又吃一片。很快地，盒子裡什麼都不剩了。

💬 都幫你整理好，不要再問了！
another　別的，其他的
the other　另一個

{ **我也不喜歡吃臭豆腐。** }

▶ either 和 neither 都有「也」的意思，用法有何差別？

🔍 你先選選看

A: I don't know how to swim.
B: Me **either / neither**.

A: 我不會游泳。
B: 我也不會。

---

A: I can't speak Taiwanese.
B: I can't **either / neither**.

A: 我不會講台語。
B: 我也不會。

Ans: neither, either

▶ either 和 neither 最大的差別在於 either 一定要和否定字搭配，而 neither 本身就帶有否定意味。

A: I've never been to Japan.
　我從沒去過日本。

B: I haven't either.
　我也沒去過。

▶ Me neither. 的説法還可以有多種變化。我們可以把 neither 放在句首，因為它是個否定字，所以後方的詞序要倒裝：

**neither + 助／ be 動詞 + 主詞**

A: I don't like stinky tofu.
　我不喜歡吃臭豆腐。

B: Neither do I.
　我也不喜歡。

都幫你整理好，不要再問了！
either → 加否定字
neither → 單獨表否定

# 我們半數的時間都花在閒聊上。

▶ 形容「半數」的形容詞 half，後面須不須接介系詞 of ？

## 你先選選看

A: Was the meeting very productive?
B: No. we spent **half / half the** time talking.

A: 那場會議有很大的進展嗎？
B: 沒有。我們半數的時間都花在閒聊上。

Ans: half the

▶ half 當「半數、一半」解釋時，句型是 half of the ＋ 名詞，通常此名詞前會有一限定詞（the、this、my 等），此時 of 常會被省略，但是 of 後若接代名詞或受詞則不可省略。

> 普通名詞

Half (of) the apples in the basket are rotten.
籃子裡半數的蘋果都壞了。

The teachers threw a Halloween party for the students, but only half of them showed up.
老師們替學生辦了場萬聖節派對，卻只有半數學生出席。

> 代名詞

多學一點，加深印象！

▶ 這邊學到了「半數」的英文該怎麼表達，那麼「幾分之幾」又該怎麼說？

1/2 → one half

2/3 → two thirds

3/4 → three fourths

▶ 只要將分母改為「序數」就好了！

Over one third of Americans believe in aliens.
超過三分之一的美國人都相信有外星人。

Two fifths is equal to forty percent.
五分之二就等於百分之四十。

# 天氣太冷，我不想洗澡。

▶ 「太…以至於…」的英文句型是什麼？

🔍 你先選選看

A: Why are there dirty dishes in the sink?
B: Sorry. I was **so / too** tired to wash the dishes last night.

A: 為什麼水槽裡有髒碗？
B: 抱歉。我昨天晚上累到沒辦法洗碗。

Ans: too

▶ 在 too...to... 的句型中， to 是作為不定詞的用法，所以後面接原形動詞。

▶ 在 so...that... 的句型中，that 後面跟的是子句。so...that... 的本身沒有否定的涵義，需有 not 配合才能成為否定句。

It's <u>too</u> cold for me <u>to</u> take a shower.
It's <u>so</u> cold <u>that</u> I don't want to take a shower.
天氣太冷，我不想洗澡。

Nick was <u>too</u> excited <u>to</u> fall asleep.
Nick was <u>so</u> excited <u>that</u> he couldn't fall asleep.
尼克太興奮，所以睡不著覺。

💬 都幫你整理好，不要再問了！
too...to...　太…以至於不能…
so...that...　如此…以至於…

# {那齣戲有點無聊。}

▶ bit 是「少量」的意思，那麼它的副詞用法「有點…」
要說 a bit 還是 one bit？

🔍 你先選選看

A: How did you like the play?
B: It was **one / a** bit dull.

A: 你覺得那齣戲怎麼樣？
B: 有點無聊。

---

A: What did you think of the movie?
B: I didn't like it **one / a** bit.

A: 你覺得那部電影如何？
B: 我一點也不喜歡。

Ans: a, one

▶ a bit 是一個表同意的片語，是「有點、有些」的意思。

The book was interesting, but a bit long.
那本書很有趣，但有點長。

▶ one bit 是用來加強語氣，強調「一點點都（不）」，具有否定意味。

I didn't believe his story—not one bit.
我不相信他說的話，一點也不。

 都幫你整理好，不要再問了！
a bit 　有點，有些
one bit 　一點都不

# 如果你用功讀書，應該可以通過考試。

▶ 「用功唸書」是 study hard 還是 study hardly?

## 你先選選看

A: If you study **hard / hardly**, you should be able to pass the exam.
B: I hope you're right.

A: 如果你用功讀書，應該可以通過考試。
B: 希望你說得沒錯。

Ans: hard

▶ 有些副詞是直接由形容詞加 ly 而來，但可不是每個副詞都可以比照辦理，像是形容詞 hard 本身就可作副詞，表「辛苦，努力，用力」的意思，而 hardly 這個副詞則完全是另一個意思，表「幾乎不」的意思。

You have to work hard to succeed.
你得要努力工作才會成功。

We could hardly afford to pay the rent.
我幾乎付不起房租。

 都幫你整理好，不要再問了！
hard 用功地，努力地
hardly 幾乎不

# 那匹馬跑了最後一名。

▶ last 和 latest，哪個才是代表「最後」的意思？

## 你先選選看

A: Did the horse you bet on win the race?
B: No. He finished **latest / last**.

A: 你下注的那匹馬有跑贏嗎？
B: 沒。牠跑最後一名。

Ans: last

▶ 在排順序或是數東西時，常會用序數 first、second、third... 等，而「最後一個」就叫做 last。

Today is Hugh's last day at work.
今天是阿休最後一天上班。

▶ late 則是指時間上晚、遲的意思。「比較晚」是 later，而 latest 則是「最新的，最近的」。

Have you read Steven King's latest novel?
你看過史蒂芬金最新的小說了嗎？

 都幫你整理好，不要再問了！

last　最後的

latest　最新的，最近的

# 他家跟城堡沒兩樣。

▶ as、like 和 alike 都有「相像，類似」的意思，用法上有何區別？

## 你先選選看

A: His house is **as / like** a castle.
B: Yeah. He must be rich.

A: 他家跟城堡沒兩樣。
B: 對啊。他一定很有錢。

---

A: Have you always been this thin?
B: No. I was chubby **as / like** a child.

A: 你一直都這麼瘦嗎？
B: 沒有啊。我小時候胖嘟嘟的。

---

A: Why don't you like this neighborhood?
B: Because all the houses are **like / alike**.

A: 你為什麼不喜歡這個社區？
B: 因為這裡所有的房子都好像。

Ans: like, as, alike

▶ like 作介系詞，後面一定要接名詞，中文就是「像…一樣」；as 與 like 的用法很像，但是後面接的通常是某種特徵或是身份，中文解釋為「身為，當作」；alike 作為形容詞或是副詞，後面不再接任何字，所以都是放在句尾。

Kevin looks just like his father.
凱文長得與他父親很像。

Tim works at the company <u>as</u> a consultant.
提姆在這家公司擔任顧問一職。

The two brothers look so <u>alike</u>.
這兩兄弟長得真像。

Not everyone thinks <u>alike</u>.
不是每個人的想法都一樣。

都幫你整理好，不要再問了！

like 像，相似

as 身為，當作

alike 相像的；相似地

# 他真是個帥哥。

▶ 什麼是複合形容詞？

🔍 你先選選看

A: Do you need anything at the grocery store?
B: Yeah. Could you get some **sun-drying / sun-dried** tomatoes for me?

A: 你需要我去超市帶點什麼嗎？
B: 要。你能幫我買點曬乾的番茄嗎？

---

A: Ryan is so handsome!
B: Yeah. He's a **good-looking / well-looking** guy.

A: 萊恩真帥！
B: 對啊。他是個帥哥。

Ans: sun-dried, good-looking

▶ 複合形容詞就是由兩個字中間加上連字號而成的形容詞，複合形容詞的兩個字有多種固定的組合方式，而跟名詞有關的複合式形容詞，例子有：

a remote-controlled robot
遙控機器人

a self-centered person
自我中心的人

▶ 有一些複合形容詞因為使用頻率非常高，所以把連字號拿掉，直接兩個字變成一個字：

> a handmade cabinet
> 手工的櫃子

> a heartbroken girl
> 心碎的女孩

▶ 複合式形容詞還可用動詞／副詞 + p.p. 的方式呈現

> a well-known actress
> 一位知名女演員

> a densely-populated city
> 一座人口密集的城市

> a cold-blooded creature
> 一種冷血動物

> an old-fashioned suit
> 一套老派的西裝

▶ 複合式形容詞還有 名詞／形容詞 + V-ing 的形態

> a mouth-watering dish
> 一道令人垂涎的菜

> an English-speaking country
> 以英文為主要語言的國家

> a good-looking boy
> 一位長相帥氣的男孩

> a long-lasting battery
> 一顆電量持久的電池

# 他可能會晚點到。

▶ 表達「可能…」時，要用 maybe 還是 may be ？

🔍 你先選選看

A: Why isn't Tom here yet?
B: He said he **maybe / may be** a little late.

A: 為什麼湯姆還沒到這裡？
B: 他説他可能會晚點到。

Ans: may be

▶ maybe 是一個副詞，意思為「或許」、「大概」，意思等同於 perhaps，通常置於句首，may be 則要用「情狀助動詞 + be 動詞」的組合，意思是「可能是」、「大概是」，置於主詞之後。

Maybe she is right.
= She may be right.
　或許她是對的。

Maybe we should just be friends.
也許我們當朋友就好。

Perhaps it will rain tomorrow.
明天可能會下雨。

💬 都幫你整理好，不要再問了！
maybe + 主詞 + 動詞
主詞 + may be...

# 帶輕便的行李就好。

▶ light 到底是修飾名詞還是動詞？

🔍 你先選選看

A: Are the extra baggage fees expensive?
B: Yes. So be sure to pack **light / lightly**.

A: 行李超重費會很貴嗎？
B: 會。所以務必帶輕便的行李就好。

Ans: light

▶ 大家都有用「形容詞修飾名詞，用副詞修飾動作」的概念，但這題算是個「很實用」的小陷阱。雖然 pack 是「打包」的動作，但從這句要表達「帶輕便的行李」（或是看中譯知道意思也行），不難明白其實 light 要修飾的根本是「行李」這個名詞，而不是「打包」這個動作，所以要選擇的是 light 而不是 lightly 了。

▶ 在字典上你會查到 light 可以當副詞，但也僅限於 travel light 或 pack light 等這種字面上看來是動詞，其實骨子裡要形容的是與該動作相關的「物品」的情況了。

▶ 而 lightly 本身則有「輕輕地」或「少量地」的意思：

She placed her hand lightly on his shoulder.
她輕輕地把手放在他的肩上。

The popcorn was lightly salted.
爆米花有加少量的鹽。

# {老年人比年輕人更需要醫療照護。

▶ 「the + 形容詞」所組成的名詞，後面出現的動詞要用單數還是複數？

🔍 你先選選看

A: Why is medical insurance for old people more expensive.
B: Because the old **need / needs** more medical care than the young.

A: 為什麼老人的醫療保險比較貴？
B: 因為老人比年輕人更需要醫療照護。

Ans: need

▶ the + 形容詞表示具有此相同特質的人。例如 the poor 就等於 the poor people，因此後面的動詞要使用複數。

The rich <u>are</u> getting richer and the poor <u>are</u> getting poorer.
富人越來越富有，窮人越來越貧困。

▶ 還有更多常見例子：

the blind　盲人
the deaf　失聰人士
the unemployed　失業人士
the homeless　遊民
the religious　信教的人
the Irish　愛爾蘭人

▶ 還是有些例外，例如 the accused（被告）、the deceased（死者）、the former（前者）、the latter（後者）等，可以指單一的人或事。

The accused was found guilty of murder.
該位被告被判謀殺罪。

The millionaire started a charity to help <u>the sick</u> and <u>the needy</u>.
那名富翁開始做慈善，幫助貧苦以及有需要的人。

Some people believe that <u>the living</u> can communicate with <u>the dead</u>.
有些人相信活人能跟死人溝通。

## { 我不是一直都這麼忙。 }

▶ not always 和 always not 的意思有何不同？

🔍 你先選選看

A: Are you always so busy?
B: No. I'm **not always / always not** this busy.

A: 你一直都這麼忙嗎？
B: 沒有。我不是一直都這麼忙。

Ans: not always

▶ 這個問題涉及到「部分否定」的概念，要表達「並非全部」、「並非每一個」、「並非總是」等，可用 not all、not every、not always 來表示。

| Not all of Spielberg's movies have been successful.
| 並非所有史匹柏的電影都很賣座。

| Meg doesn't always like to help with housework.
| 梅格不是一直都喜歡幫忙做家事。

| It's not every day that you see a surfing dog.
| 你不是每天都可以看到狗狗在衝浪。

▶如果要表達「全部否定」，那就直接用帶有否定意味的 none、never 等字即可，在極少數的狀況下才會說 all not、every not、always not。

**None** of the author's books has been successful.
這個作者的書沒一本是暢銷的。

Jennifer **never** comes to work on time.
珍妮佛上班從沒準時過。

**Nobody** could answer my question.
沒人能回答我的問題。

**Nothing** beats a cold beer on a hot day.
沒什麼能比得上在大熱天裡來杯冰啤酒。

There's **nowhere** I'd rather be than here.
對我來說沒有任何一處比這裡更好了。

# 形容詞 & 副詞總複習

請選出適當的答案

1. He's _____ as successful as his brother.

    A. not

    B. so

    C. no

    D. isn't

2. She finished the test in _____ time than I did.

    A. fewer

    B. little

    C. few

    D. less

3. I enjoyed the show _____ much.

    A. really

    B. very

    C. well

    D. real

4. The cherry trees are blooming _____ this year.

    A. lately

    B. latest

    C. late

    D. last

5. Tom can't ride a bike, and I can't _____.

    A. neither

    B. either

    C. nor

    D. also

6. She doesn't drink coffee and _____ do I.

   A. not

   B. either

   C. neither

   D. also

7. The students all dress _____ .

   A. like

   B. alike

   C. same

   D. likely

8. My doctor examined one eye, and then _____ .

   A. the other

   B. other

   C. others

   D. another

9. Kathy only dates _____ guys.

   A. good-looking

   B. looking-good

   C. look-well

   D. well-looking

10. He didn't enjoy the trip _____ bit.

   A. little

   B. a

   C. one

   D. any

解答

1. A   2. D   3. B   4. C   5. B

6. C   7. B   8. A   9. A   10. C

# *Chapter 3*
# 冠詞
# *Articles*

冠詞的惱人之處：

因為中文幾乎不強調冠詞，概念較為抽象，比較難用中文語法去聯想該用什麼冠詞。

不定冠詞 a / an 和定冠詞 the 超難分！有些名詞前甚至不用加冠詞，限制一大堆，雖然只是小小一個字，只要用錯，意思天差地遠，考試也超常被扣分！

a 和 an 是以後面的名詞是否為母音開頭來決定用法，但偏偏有些字看起來不像母音開頭，一定得知道正確發音才能判別。

# 冠詞大哉問
## Questions About Using Article

冠詞的作用到底是什麼？不能只固定用一個字就好了嗎，還要分 a、an 和 the，有夠麻煩！

首先大家要有一個觀念，你現在學的是「英文」，可不是中文，當然不能用中文的思維去看待英文文法啊！用最簡白的話來說，冠詞是用來告訴別人所指的到底是「特定事物」還是「一般事物」。比方說：

He's a boy.
他是個男孩

He's the boy I like.
他就是我喜歡的那個男孩。

第一句的中文只是要講出該人是男孩這件事，是很普遍的敘述，但第二句則是特指「我曾經提過的」那位男孩，將名詞作了限定，因此用冠詞 the。a 在中文裡常常可不翻出，「他是一個男孩」也可說成「他是男孩」，但英文句子裡則一定要有冠詞，不然就犯了文法上的錯誤。

雖然用慣中文的我們常會覺得要判斷要用什麼冠詞很麻煩，但其實像西班牙文、法文等歐洲語言也很注重冠詞的用法，而且變化還更多咧！弄清楚定冠詞與不定冠詞的概念，除了搞定英文，學其他外文語法也比較輕鬆喔！

冠詞一定要加在名詞前面，不可以單獨存在嗎？

冠詞本身幾乎不具意義，一定要搭配名詞出現才可以，且還跟名詞的屬性密切相關，例如某些專有名詞前一定要加定冠詞：

the Mississippi 密西西比 →地名
the Johnsons 強森一家 →代表家族的姓氏名稱

當然還有更多特殊的用法，有時多看報章雜誌就更能意會哪些特定名詞必須加冠詞，哪些不用。

有沒有完全不能加冠詞的名詞？

有一些名詞前面不加冠詞，稱為「零冠詞」，例如：

I've been learning the Japanese for five years.
我日文學了五年了。

這裡的 Japanese 指的是「日本語」，為學科名稱，前面不需加 the。（但若指的是「日本人」，就要加冠詞）

還有我們常提到的「從事某運動」：

Jason plays ~~the~~ badminton every
weekend.
傑森每個週末都會打羽毛球。

　　舉凡打籃球、排球等運動項目，前面也
都不需加 the。

　　此外，「三餐」、「季節」、「日期」、
「顏色」等名詞也是一樣，前面不加冠詞：

I'm starving because I didn't eat ~~the~~
breakfast this morning.
我餓得要死，因為我今天早上沒吃早餐。

Sandy gave a present to her
teacher on ~~the~~ Teacher's Day.
珊蒂在教師節時送了一份禮物給她的老師。

The women in ~~the~~ black looks
gorgeous.
那個穿黑衣的女人看起來美極了。

# { 你有機會應該試吃看看那家餐廳。 }

▶ 「有機會做某事」要說 have a chance to... 還是 have the chance to... ？

🔍 你先選選看

A: Did you have **a / the** chance to look at that report I gave you?
B: Not yet. But I should have time this afternoon.

A: 你有機會看看我交給你的那篇報告嗎？
B: 還沒。不過我今天下午應該會有時間。

Ans: a

▶ 表示「有機會、時機做某事」時，若是此機會僅有一次，是特定的狀況時，用 have / get the chance to V：

John <u>had the chance</u> to work in the U.S., but he passed on it.
約翰有機會去美國工作，不過他放棄了那個機會。

▶ 但若此種機會有多次發生的可能性，就用 have / get a chance to V。

You should try that restaurant when you <u>get a chance</u>.
你有機會應該試吃看看那家餐廳。

💬 都幫你整理好，不要再問了！

have / get the chance to V → 指特定機會或僅止一次

have / get a chance to V → 機會出現多次

# {我從沒遇過拿中華民國護照的外國人。}

▶ 定冠詞何時要用 a？何時要用 an？

A: I've never met a foreigner with **a / an** ROC passport before.
B: I'm a citizen, so I'm not a foreigner.

A: 我從沒遇過拿中華民國護照的外國人。
B: 我是本國國民，不是外國人。

Ans: an

▶ 大家都知道冠詞 a 後面的名詞若開頭字母是 a、e、i、o、u 其中一個母音，冠詞就要改變成 an，譬如：an umbrella、an egg，但其實冠詞 a 和 an 變化的原則並不單純是靠看到的字母決定的，而是跟「發音」有關。

▶ 所以要辨別用 a 還是 an，最正確的觀念應該是：若冠詞後面單字開頭是「母音發音」的要用 an，是「子音發音」的要用 a，譬如：an hour [aʊr]、a United [juˈnaɪtɪd] States citizen。此題冠詞後面接的是母音發音開頭的字母 R [ɑr]，所以要用 an 而不是 a。

# 我要去郵局寄封信。

▶ 名詞前面到底什麼時候要加 the ？

## 你先選選看

A: Is that **a / the** guy you were telling me about?
B: No. That's a different guy.

A: 那是你跟我說的那個男的嗎？
B: 不是。那是另一個人。

---

A: Where are you headed?
B: I'm going to **the / X** post office to mail a letter.

A: 你要去哪裡？
B: 我要去郵局寄封信。

Ans: the, the

在很多狀況下，名詞前通常會加 the，以下就幫你整理一些常見的例子，其實用久了就會了，不用死記：

▶ 如果提到前面說過的名詞，再次提到的時候，名詞前要加 the，有點像是中文在講「那個…」。

A: I heard on the news that a man was attacked by a bear.
我聽新聞說有一個人被熊攻擊。

B: Is the man still alive?
那人還活著嗎？

→ 說話者和聽話者都知道在說誰，因為前面有提過。

▶ 表達形容詞或副詞的最高級時，前面要加 the。

That's the biggest lobster I've ever seen.
這是我看過最大的龍蝦。

Bobby is the worst student in our class.
波比是我們班上最差的學生。

▶ 公司行號、博物館、動物園等機構或建築，前面要加 the。

I went to the bank to make a deposit.
我去銀行存錢。

The United Nations is headquartered in New York.
聯合國總部在紐約。

▶ 醫院名稱前不加 the。

The patient was taken to Bellevue Hospital.
那名病患被送到貝爾維尤醫院就診。

▶ 在國家（country）、城市（city）、州（state）前不可加冠詞，
但是某些特定字組合成國家的名稱時，前面要加 the。

The capital of Taiwan is Taipei.
台灣的首都是台北。

There are fifty states in the United States.
美國有五十五州。

▶ 在河流（river），海洋（ocean, sea），沙漠
（desert）前要加 the，不過像是湖泊（lake）
或山脈（mountain）前面，單數時不加冠詞，
複數時要加 the。

Mount St. Helens erupted in 1980.
聖海倫火山在 1980 年爆發。

The Great Lakes were formed during the last ice age.
五大湖是在上次冰河期形成的。

# {我的湯裡有一隻蒼蠅。}

▶ 定冠詞 a / an 表示「單數」，那 one 也表示單數，
用法上有什麼不一樣嗎？可以互相代換嗎？

🔍 你先選選看

A: Waiter, there's **a / one** fly in my soup.
B: I'm so sorry, sir. I'll bring you another bowl.

A: 服務生，我的湯裡有一隻蒼蠅。
B: 不好意思，先生。我會換一碗給你。

---

A: How many lumps of sugar do you want in your coffee?
B: Just <u>**a / one**</u> lump, please.

A: 你的咖啡要加幾顆糖？
B: 只要一顆就好，麻煩了。

Ans: a, one

▶ 雖然看到名詞前有 a 就代表單數，但跟中文不太一樣，中文有時會省略定冠詞，
例如「他是一位老師」，中文也可說成「他是老師」而不講出「一位」這個量詞。
英文的 a 可萬萬不能省，一定要說 He's <u>a</u> teacher. 不能說 He's teacher。

Is that <u>a</u> fountain pen?
那是一支鋼筆嗎？

▶ one 可以當形容詞或代名詞來用，主要有「強調數量為一」的意味。

Our dog is <u>one</u> year old.
我的狗一歲大。

If I could afford a sports car, I'd buy <u>one</u>.
如果我買得起跑車，我就會買一台。

▶ 再來想想這兩句的差別吧：

I have <u>a</u> sister who lives in Boston.
我有一個住在波士頓的姊姊。

I have <u>one</u> sister.
我有一個姊姊。

▶ 第一句用的 a 只是句中必備的冠詞，並無強調數量的意味，第二句則是很明顯地強調我只有「一位」姊妹，感受出這兩個用法的差異了嗎？

# 我昨晚半夜才上床睡覺。

在「早上」、「中午」、「下午」，前面要加 the 嗎？

A: What time does your flight arrive?
B: At eight in **X / the** morning.

A: 你的班機什麼時候到。
B: 早上八點。

---

A: Why are you so tired?
B: I went to bed at **X / the** midnight last night.

A: 你為什麼這麼累？
B: 我昨晚半夜才上床睡覺。

Ans: the, X

▶ 這個問題雖然基本，但很多人都會搞不清楚，在早上（morning）、下午（afternoon）、傍晚（evening）前要加 the，但是晚上（night），中午（noon），午夜（midnight）前不加 the。

I usually take a nap in the afternoon.
我通常下午會睡午覺。

What time do you wake up in the morning?
你早上幾點起床？

In the evenings, we like to relax at home.
我們晚上喜歡在家休息放輕鬆。

The festival starts at noon tomorrow.
節慶從明天中午開始。

# { 你已經工作了，還是還在上學？ }

▶ 「上學」到底是 go to school 還是 go to the school?

▶ 「上學」要說 go to school，不過若是說 go to the school，則意為「去學校」，可以是去某間學校參加活動、參觀等，不限定是學生去「上學」。

If you don't go to college, you'll never find a good job.
如果你不上大學，你永遠也找不到好工作。

We're going to the school to attend a lecture.
我們要去學校聽演講。

▶ 另一個類似的片語就是 go to church。go to church 是「上教堂作禮拜」的意思，而 go to the church 則是單純指「前往教堂」，不一定是從事宗教活動。

Do you go to church every Sunday?
你每個星期天都會去做禮拜嗎？

I went to the church to hear the choir perform.
我去教堂聽唱詩班表演。

# 冠詞總複習

請選填冠詞 a、an 或 the

1. 那隻鴨子孵了一顆蛋。

   The duck laid _____ egg.

2. 那就是我跟你提過的那個女孩。

   That's _____ girl I was telling you about.

3. 你可以借我一支筆嗎？

   Do you have _____ pen I can borrow?

4. 可以麻煩你把鹽遞給我嗎？

   Could you please pass _____ salt?

5. 我哥是一位醫生。

   My brother is _____ doctor.

6. 讀那篇故事花了我一小時。

   It took me _____ hour to read the story.

7. 我們在動物園裡看到了一隻大象。

   We saw _____ elephant at the zoo.

8. 羅伯是我認識最聰明的人。

   Robert is _____ smartest person I know.

9. 我們女兒想要一隻小狗作為聖誕禮物。

   Our daughter wants _____ puppy for Christmas.

10. 你在海灘玩得開心嗎？

    Did you have fun at _____ beach?

# Chapter 4
# 動詞
# Verbs

動詞為何如此惱人？

同一個動詞，卻會因後面接的是 Ving（動名詞）或 to V（不定詞）
而產生語意上的差異，用錯誤會就大了！
I stopped playing computer games for three days.
我停止玩電腦遊戲三天。
I stopped to play computer games for three days.
我停下來（原本在做的事），玩了三天的電腦遊戲。

並不是所有動詞後面都可以加 to V，有少數動詞後面只能加 Ving！
如 suggest、avoid、enjoy 等，許多人常常 to V 和 Ving 混用，這樣
是錯的。

# 動詞大哉問
## *Questions About Using Verbs*

動詞啊動詞,你的變化也太多了吧!我真的猜不透你,你到底有幾張臉啊?

　　動詞向來是讓人最感頭痛的詞類,牽涉到眾多文法概念,無論是時態、主動被動、或是其後該接什麼詞,都需要花腦筋去記憶,其實很少有人會單獨將動詞抓出來學,大多都要配合其他文法概念做變化。但無論如何,最起碼要做到能夠及時反應正確的動詞三態,不然就算背了再多動詞,三態寫錯也是枉然。好在大部份的動詞變化還算有規則,過去式就加 ed,過去分詞大多加 en,只有少數比較例外,像是以下這些:

　　原形動詞→過去式→過去分詞

drink → drank → drunk

run → ran → run

take → took → taken

wear → wore → worn

fall → fell → fallen

cut → cut → cut

fight → fought → fought

shine → shone → shone

　　當然,除了上述這些之外還有更多不規則變化,只能靠多看、多背來記憶,不過熟記這些常用的動詞變化,起碼不會寫出像是 I "runned" away. 這種可笑的句子吧!接下來的問題,就是怎麼正確地使用它們了。

我動詞三態已經背得滾瓜爛熟,但重點是怎麼用啊?而且似乎變化還不只有這麼多而已,還看過加 ing、以及前面加 to 的原形動詞…太惱人了,我搞不懂!

　　恭喜你!熟記動詞三態對文法學習者來説可是最基本的,有了基本功,就可以再往下學更多東西。

　　你剛提到的「Ving」、「to + 原形動詞」,這些都是「披著動詞皮的其他詞類」。Ving 的正式名稱叫做「動名詞」,體會一下,它到底該算是動詞還是名詞哩?

**Playing basketball is my favorite activity.**

(打籃球是我最愛的活動。)

　　我們都知道一個句子不能在沒有任何連接詞的情況下,出現兩個動詞,在這句子中,已經有 be 動詞 is 了(be 動詞也是動詞的一種喔,別忘了!)那麼 playing 應該算是「名詞」才對,指的是打籃球「這件事」。

　　看完以上例句,比較有感覺了嗎?動詞

除了扮演它原本的角色，還可演變成動名詞、不定詞、分詞等三種不同的動狀詞。動狀詞在句子中雖看起來像動詞，卻被借來扮演名詞、形容詞，或副詞，因此動狀詞必須被視為別的詞性。

## 什麼是及物動詞？不及物動詞？

及物動詞就是「會接受詞的動詞」，不及物動詞就是「後面可不接東西的動詞」，用中文解釋你就可以理解了，例如我們中文不可能會說「我正在看。」這樣就算一個句子了，一定會說「我正在看電視」、「我正在看書」，會有一個接受該動作的受詞，而且中間不用加介系詞，這種動詞就叫及物動詞：

I watched. (X)

I watched the show last night. ( ○ )
　　　　　　　→ 受詞

反之，不用接受詞的就是不及物動詞，例如：

The wind is blowing.
風正在吹。

We are laughing.
我們正在笑。

及物與不及物還會更進一步分為完全與不完全及物…等，建議學到的時候都用例句來記憶，比較不會錯亂。

# 我發現我男友劈腿。

▶ 表「發現」的 found 何時會搭配介系詞，變成 found out 這個片語？

## 你先選選看

A: Why did you break up with your boyfriend?
B: I **found / found out** he was cheating on me.

A: 妳為什麼和妳男友分手？
B: 我發現他劈腿。

Ans: found out

▶ 英文中表達「發現」某人或某物的狀態，可以用 find 或 find out 來表示，兩者的句型分述如下：

find + 受詞 + 形容詞片語（作受詞補語）

Jack woke up to find his bedroom ankle-deep in water.
傑克醒來發現他的臥室水深及踝。

find out + that 子句

When did you find out that you were a dopted?
你是何時發現自己是被領養的？

多學一點，加深印象！

▶ find 主要是指「找到一件你正在找的東西」，而 find out 多指「發現」事物，例如藉由閱讀、觀察或搜尋，進而獲得新的資訊。

| Can you help me find my keys?
| 你能幫我找找我的鑰匙嗎？

| Kelly's parents found out that she had a boyfriend.
| 凱莉的爸媽發現她交男友了。

▶ find 和 find out 也可互通，但通常是用在比較正式的情況下：

| The study found that some chemicals can cause skin cancer.
| 研究發現某些化學物質可能會導致皮膚癌。

# 你有去看攝影展嗎？

▶ 有時會看到 come 或 go 後面直接接另一個原形動詞，一個句子不是不能將兩個動詞放在一起嗎？

🔍 你先選選看

A: Be sure to come **visiting / visit** me next time you're in town.
B: OK, I will.

A: 下次到市區來的時候一定要來看我喔。
B: 好，我會的。

Ans: visit

▶ 一般來說，兩個原形動詞是不能直接放在一起的，但 come 和 go 這兩個字卻是例外。

▶ 原本應該是 come / go and V... 但在口語中，中間的 and 常被省略，因此變成 come / go V。

Did you <u>go (and) see</u> the photography exhibit?
你有去看攝影展嗎？

Could you <u>come help</u> me with my homework?
你能來幫我寫功課嗎？

💬 都幫你整理好，不要再問了！
come / go + 原形動詞　來／去做某事

# 你該去唸書了。

▶ 什麼情況下，should 後面會加 be Ving？

🔍 你先選選看

A: Is that book interesting?
B: Yes. You should **be reading / read** it.

A: 那本書有趣嗎？
B: 有趣啊。你真該看一下。

A: Can I watch TV?
B: No. You should **be studying / study**.

A: 我可以看電視嗎？
B: 不行。你該去唸書。

Ans: read, be studying

▶ 助動詞 should 最基本的用法就是其後直接接原形動詞，表示建議對方應該做某事；should 接現在進行式，則是強調這件事應該「馬上進行」。

You should <u>find</u> a better job.
你應該找個更好的工作。

You should <u>call</u> your parents more often.
你應該更常打電話

You should <u>be doing</u> your homework.
你現在應該去做回家作業。

You shouldn't <u>be driving</u> so fast.
你不應該開這麼快。

 都幫你整理好，不要再問了！

should ＋ 原 V → 表達建議，指現在或未來該做的事。

should ＋ be ＋ Ving → 強調此刻應該馬上進行的動作。

# 她以前不喜歡我，但現在喜歡了。

▶ used to 和 be used to，到底哪個才是「習慣」？

▶ 表示「習慣」，可說 be used to +N / Ving；而 used to + 原形動詞，意思是「過去…」之意。

I used to drink coffee, but now I drink tea.
我以前都喝咖啡，現在改喝茶了。

She didn't use to like me, but now she does.
她以前不喜歡我，但現在喜歡。

I'm used to waking up early now.
我現在習慣早起了。

多學一點，加深印象！

**get used to　逐漸習慣**

The food is spicy, but you get used to it.
食物很辣，但你會習慣的。

都幫你整理好，不要再問了！
主詞 + used to + 原 V
→「過去…（現在已非如此）」
主詞 + be + used to + 名詞或動名詞
（Ving）→習慣…

# 麥可考慮要轉換工作跑道。

▶ 動詞 consider（考慮）後面要接不定詞還是動名詞？

## 你先選選看

A: Cars are so expensive these days.
B: Have you considered **to buy / buying** a used car?

A: 汽車現在好貴。
B: 你有考慮要買中古車嗎？

Ans: buying

▶ 中文常說「考慮要去…（做某事）」，因此很多人以為在 consider（考慮）的後面接的是不定詞 to V，這是一個常見的錯誤。事實上，consider 後面要接動名詞 Ving 才對。

| Michael is considering changing careers.
| 麥可考慮要轉換工作跑道。

▶ 順便補充 consider 的另一個意思，表「視為，當作」，通常用被動語態。

| Descartes is considered the father of modern philosophy.
| 笛卡爾被視為現代哲學之父。

多學一點，加深印象！

▶ consider 當「視為，當作」的意思時，句型可為：
consider + 名詞 + (to be) + 受詞補語
名詞 + is / are considered + (to be) + 受詞補語

Many consider Messi (to be) the best soccer player in the world.
許多人認為梅西是世上最棒的足球員。

Wigs were considered fashionable in colonial America.
在美洲殖民時期，人們認為假髮很時髦。

# 請回避管制區。

▶ 動詞 avoid（避免）後面的動詞要用原形動詞還是動名詞？

## 你先選選看

A: Is that area safe at night?
B: No. You should avoid **walk / walking** there after dark.

A: 那一區晚上安全嗎？
B: 不安全。你入夜後要避免在那裡行走。

Ans: walking

▶ avoid 這個動詞表示「避免」、「防止」不好的事情發生。後面只能接名詞，當句子中有第二個動詞出現時，必須改成動名詞，意思是指「避免某些不利的處境或狀況」。

→ 動名詞
Please avoid entering off-limit areas.

Please avoid off-limit areas.
請避免進入管制區。
→ 名詞

都幫你整理好，不要再問了！
avoid + Ving　避免（做某事）

# { 你如果在乎自己的健康，就該停止吸菸。 }

▶ 「停止某動作」或是「停止現在的動作，轉而進行別的動作」，這兩者的英文要怎麼表達？

🔍 你先選選看

A: If you care about your health, you should stop **smoking / to smoke**.
B: I'm trying to quit, but it's really hard.

A: 你如果在乎自己的健康，就該停止吸菸。
B: 我很努力戒，但真的很難。

---

A: I think I see a gas station up ahead.
B: Good. Let's stop **getting / to get** gas.

A: 我好像看到前面有一家加油站。
B: 好極了。我們停下來加油吧。

Ans: smoking, to get

▶ 句子裡有兩個動詞出現時，通常要將其中一個動詞改成不定詞（to + V）或是動名詞（Ving）。某些動詞後固定只能接動名詞用，如 enjoy、keep、mind 等，某些只能接不定詞，譬如 decide、want、need 等，基本上只有用法上的差別，意思並不會改變。不過 stop 這個動詞比較特別，後面可接 to + V 或 Ving，但是意義不同：

I should stop to eat.
我應該停下來去吃點東西。（而非停止吃東西）

The girl finally stopped crying.
這個女孩終於不哭了。

💬 都幫你整理好，不要再問了！
stop + to + V 停下來去做另一件事
stop + Ving 停止做某事

# 我爸媽希望我每科都拿 A。

▶ 表「期待」或「預料」的動詞 expect 後面接的動詞要用什麼形態？

## 你先選選看

A: Are your parents very demanding?
B: Yes. They expect me **get / to get** straight As in school.

A: 你的父母會很嚴苛嗎？
B: 會啊。他們希望我每科都拿 A。

Ans: to get

▶ expect 作及物動詞時，中文解釋是「期待，預期」，後面可以直接接名詞，也可接 that + 子句。

We're expecting good weather tomorrow.
我們認為明天會有好天氣。

Economists expect (that) the economy will improve.
經濟學家預測經濟將會好轉。

▶ 要求／期望某人做某事，可用 expect sb. to do sth. 表示。

The boss expects his employees to be on time.
這名老闆要求他的員工要準時上班。

多學一點，加深印象！

▶ 提到 expect 這個字，很多人都會拼錯，寫成介系詞 except（除…之外），切記下次不要再寫錯啦！

The museum is open every day except Tuesday.
那間博物館每天都開，除了週二。

💬 都幫你整理好，不要再問了！
expect sb. to do sth. →要求／指望某人會做某事
expect（that）+ 子句→ 預料到（某事）

## { 離開時別忘了鎖門。 }

▶ forget 和 remember 後面接動名詞或不定詞，意思上有什麼差別？

🔍 你先選選看

A: Don't forget **locking / to lock** the door when you leave.
B: OK. I won't.

A: 離開時別忘了鎖門。
B: 好的。我不會忘記的。

---

A: How could you forget **meeting / to meet** him?
B: It was a long time ago, and I have a bad memory.

A: 你怎麼會忘了你曾經見過他？
B: 那是很久之前的事了，而且我記性不好。

Ans: to lock, meeting

▶ 若是忘記／記得要去做某事，則後面動詞要用不定詞；若是忘記／記得曾經做過的事，後面就用動名詞：

Patricia forgot <u>to go</u> to the post office.
派翠夏忘記去郵局。

Did you remember <u>to buy</u> milk on the way home?
你回家時有記得順便買牛奶嗎？

Patricia forgot <u>going</u> to the post office.
派翠夏忘記她去過郵局了。

I'll never forget <u>watching</u> the birth of my son.
我永遠忘不了看我兒子出生的那一幕。

💬 都幫你整理好，不要再問了！
forget / remember + to V.
→忘記、記得要…（去做某事）
forget / remember + Ving
→忘記、記得曾經…（做了什麼）

# 我老闆不會讓我請假的。

▶ 「准許某人做某事」動詞要用 let，其後的動詞要用什麼形態？

## 你先選選看

A: Are you coming to the game with us?
B: No. My boss wouldn't let me **take / to take** the day off.

A: 你要和我們一起去看球賽嗎？
B: 沒有。我老闆不讓我請假。

Ans: take

▶ let 為使役動詞，後面的動詞必須為原形，不加不定詞 to。其他常見的使役動詞還有 make、have 等。

Do your parents <u>let</u> you <u>stay</u> out late?
你父母准你晚回家嗎？

▶ 其他因為語意相近而容易混淆的動詞如 want（希望）、ask（要求）等，則要注意後面的動詞是要加上不定詞 to 的。

<u>Ask</u> your dad <u>to help</u> you with your homework.
叫你爸爸幫你做功課。

💬 都幫你整理好，不要再問了！
let + 人 + 原形動詞　讓某人做某事

# 我會叫我哥去機場接你。

▶ 使役動詞後面一般是接原形動詞，何時會接 p.p.？

🔍 你先選選看

A: Are you going to do your own taxes?
B: No. I'm going to have them **done / to do** by an accountant.

A: 你要自己報稅嗎？
B: 不要。我要請一位會計來搞定。

Ans: done

▶ 遇到這種看似你主動要做，但其實那個動作是要讓別人完成，而不是真的自己做的時候，英文都得在 p.p. 前面加上 have，變成 have + sth. + p.p. 的句型，而 have / 在這樣的句型中就被稱做「使役動詞」啦！

▶ 有沒有使役動詞在英文差別非常大，譬如有個老外朋友打電話問你在幹嘛，而你正在車廠裡洗車，就要說 I'm having my car washed.，若說 I'm washing my car. 人家會認為是你自己在洗車，雖然中文都只會回答「我在洗車」，但英文可要「講清楚」，否則你想講的意思聽在老外耳裡可能意思會完全相反！使役動詞還有另一種常見用法 have + sb. + 動詞原形，把 p.p. 動詞改成原形，就變成「指使某人做事」。

I'll have my brother pick you up at the airport.
我會叫我哥哥去機場接你。

have / get sth. / sb. + p.p

Janice got her hair dyed at the beauty parlor.
珍妮斯去髮廊染頭髮。

The woman had her husband arrested for domestic violence.
那名婦女讓她老公因家暴被逮。

都幫你整理好，不要再問了！

have / get + 事物 +p.p　讓某物（被）…

have / get + 人 + 原形動詞　叫某人去做…

# 你曾經後悔沒上大學嗎？

▶ 表「後悔、懊悔」的動詞 regret，後面的動詞該用何種形態？

🔍 你先選選看

A: Do you ever regret **moving / to move** out to California?
B: No. It was the best decision I ever made.

A: 你有沒有後悔搬到加州？
B: 沒有。那是我做過最好的決定。

Ans: moving

▶ regret 當「後悔、懊悔」時，後方就直接加上那一件事情，所以通常不是名詞（或 that 引導的名詞子句），就是動名詞。對話中的 regret 就是當「後悔」的意思，所以要用 moving。

Do you ever regret not going to college?
你曾經後悔沒上大學嗎？

▶ regret 只有在 I regret to say / inform / tell you that...「很遺憾要説／通知／告訴你…」這個説法，後方才會加 to V。這是比較正式的説法，這裡的 I regret 也可以用 I'm sorry 代替。

We regret to inform you that we've offered the position to another candidate.
很遺憾通知你，我們已經把這個職位給另一位應徵者了。

💬 都幫你整理好，不要再問了！
regret + Ving　後悔（做…）
regret + to V　遺憾地（告知對方訊息）

116

# 你喜歡做菜嗎？

▶ 有哪些動詞後面要接動名詞？

A: Do you enjoy **to cook / cooking**?
B: Well, it's better than washing the dishes.

A: 你喜歡做菜嗎？
B: 這個嘛，總比洗碗好吧。

Ans: cooking

▶ 英文的動詞比中文麻煩許多，有的後面可以直接加名詞，有的要先加介系詞，有的後面加動詞要補上 to，有些則用 -ing 的形式，最好能配合例句一起學習。像這篇中的 enjoy 後面接的動詞就要用 -ing。

▶ 其他類似動詞還有 practice、finish、mind：

I practice playing the piano every day.
我每天練習彈鋼琴。

Did you finish writing the report?
你的報告寫完了嗎？

Would you mind not smoking?
你可不可以不要抽菸？

# 那宗槍擊案的新聞真是令人震驚。

▶ shock 和 shocking 有何不同？

A: The news about that shooting was so **shocked / shocking**.
B: Yeah. I was **shocked / shocking** when I heard about it.

A: 那個槍擊的新聞真是令人震驚。
B: 對啊。我聽到的時候很驚訝。

Ans: shocking / shocked

▶ 許多表達「感覺」的動詞，後面加上 ed 或 ing 即可變成「形容詞」。如果主詞是「被動地」因為外物而產生的感覺（因…而感到），就用過去分詞 -ed。相反地，如果主詞是「主動地」散發出一種氣氛和特質，就用現在分詞 -ing。

The professor's lecture today was so boring.
那個教授今天上的課好無聊。

▶ 其他用法相似的動詞還有 surprise、amaze、excite、bore、annoy……等。

I was so bored in class that I almost fell asleep.
我上課太無聊，都快睡著了。

# 修車花了我兩千元。

▶ cost、spend、take 都有「花費」之意，意思及用法有何不同？

🔍 你先選選看

A: Is it expensive to fly there?
B: A round-trip ticket **costs / spends** around 800 dollars.

A: 坐飛機到那裡很貴嗎？
B: 來回機票大概要花八百元。

Ans: costs

## spend　花費，耗費

▶ 用於表示花錢或花時間，主詞一定是人。後面可接 Ving 或 on + N。

Roger spent 500 dollars buying Christmas presents for his kids.
羅傑花五百元買耶誕禮物給他的孩子們。

## cost　花費

it／事物 + cost（＋人）+ 金額 + to + V

It cost me two thousand dollars to get my car fixed.
修車花了我兩千元。

## take　花時間

it／事物 + take（＋人）+ 時間 + to + V

How long does it take to drive from San Francisco to San Diego?
從舊金山開車到聖地牙哥需要多久？

# 他看起來有點悲傷。

▶ 連綴動詞的用法與一般動詞有何不同？

A: How did Michael seem when you saw him?
B: He seemed a little **sadly / sad**.

A: 你看到麥可的時候，他看起來如何？
B: 他看起來有點悲傷。

Ans: sad

▶ seem 當動詞，表示「看起來像，似乎」：

Daniel seems to be doing well in school.
丹尼爾似乎在學校表現很好。

▶ 當連綴動詞，像 be 動詞一樣直接接形容詞在後面。常見的連綴動詞有：seem、feel、look、smell、sound、taste、become 等等。

Catherine's new boyfriend seems nice.
凱薩琳的新男友好像人很好。

▶ 另外，連綴動詞還可接 like，然後再加名詞或子句。

Skydiving at night doesn't seem like a good idea.
夜間跳傘似乎不是個好主意。

💬 都幫你整理好，不要再問了！
連綴動詞 + 形容詞
連綴動詞 + 名詞／子句

# 我懂了。

▶ 常在對話中聽到 get it，請問是什麼意思？

🔍 你先選選看

A: My number is 537-6874.
B: **Caught / Got** it. I'll call you back in a minute.

A: 我的電話是 537-6874。
B: 知道了。我等等再回撥給你。

Ans: Got

▶ get it 的意思是「聽到了」、「知道了」、「懂了」。在問別人的時候，常把 Do you 省略，直接說：Get it?（ it 語調上揚）；而回答的人就會用過去式的 Got it. 來表示「已經」懂了、知道了，同樣省略主詞 I。因此這裡要選過去式的 Got it.

| (Do you) get it?
| 你懂了嗎？

| (I) got it.
| 我懂了。

# 我爸媽說我必須十點前到家。

▶ 英文中，表達「必須」會用到 must / need to / have to 這三種說法，適用時機為何？

## 你先選選看

A: Is this letter urgent?
B: No. You **mustn't / don't need to** type it now.

A: 這封信很急嗎？
B: 沒有。你不必現在就打好。

Ans: don't need to

---

▶ 在一般情況下，must、need to、have to 這三者的意思差別不大，只是 must 和 have to 的語氣比較強烈，通常可用來表達「硬性規定或規矩」，或是用來強調某事的「重要性」，而 need to 則較為彈性，比較沒有「非做不可」的感覺。

> You <u>must</u> answer all the questions on the test.
> 你必須回答考卷上的所有問題。

> My parents said I <u>have to</u> be home by ten.
> 我爸媽說我必須十點前到家。

> I <u>need to</u> talk to you about something.
> 我有件事得跟你談談。

▶ 在一開始這則對話實例中，說話者想要表達的是「不必」現在就把信打出來，並沒有強烈禁止的意思，因此答案要選 don't need to。

▶ 再多看兩個例子會更清楚：

Our teacher said we mustn't lie.
我們老師叮囑我們不准說謊。

You don't have to come if you don't want to.
如果你不想來的話就不用來了。

都幫你整理好，不要再問了！

must　必須、一定要（態度強烈）

musn't　禁止，不准

have to / need to　必須

don't have to / don't need to　不必

## 參觀動物園後，我們帶孩子去吃冰淇淋。

在省略主詞的句子中，連接詞後的動詞要用什麼形態？

### 你先選選看

A: Where did you go after the zoo?
B: After **visited / visiting** the zoo, we took the kids for ice cream.

A: 你去完動物園後去了哪裡？
B: 參觀完動物園後，我們帶孩子去吃冰淇淋。

Ans: visiting

▶ 此處的 after 為連接詞，句型為：

　After ＋ S ＋ V..., S ＋ V...
＝ After ＋ Ving..., S ＋ V...

（記得前後主詞必須一致，才可以做此變化）

> After John had dinner, he watched his favorite show.
> 約翰吃完晚餐後看了他最愛的節目。

> After graduating from law school, Kevin joined a law firm.
> 法學院畢業後，凱文就到律師事務所上班。

▶ 這種寫法稱為「副詞子句的簡化」，讓同一個主詞不要一再出現，所以把主詞和 be 動詞一起省略，至於像 before（在…之前）、after（在…之後）這類有意思的連接詞要保留，但像 while、when、because 這種連接詞拿掉後並不影響意思傳遞，語意還是很明顯，因此可以省略。

Before going out, I always watch the weather report.
我外出之前都會先看氣象報告。

Because Kevin had nothing better to do, he sat around watching TV.
= Having nothing better to do, Kevin sat around watching TV.
凱文因為沒什麼更好的事可做，所以他就坐著看電視。

# 你可以幫我洗碗嗎？

▶ 動詞片語 help with 是什麼意思？
▶ help oneself to 又是什麼意思？

## 你先選選看

A: Could you help me **with / to** the dishes?
B: Sure. I'll wash if you dry.

A: 你可以幫我洗碗嗎？
B: 好啊。我洗，你來擦乾。

---

A: Please help yourself **with / to** seconds.
B: No thanks. I'm pretty full.

A: 想再吃請自己拿。
B: 不了，謝謝。我很飽。

Ans: with, to

▶ 「help 人 with」事物，是指「在某事上幫助某人」；而「help oneself to 事物」則是一個固定用法，表示「請對方自行取用…」。

Can you help me with my homework?
你可以幫我寫功課嗎？

Help yourself to some cookies.
你自己拿些餅乾來吃吧！

都幫你整理好，不要再問了！
help 人 with 事物　幫助某人做某事
help oneself + to + 事物　自行取用……

# 我建議你去法國念一年書。

▶ recommend 和 suggest 這類表「建議」的動詞，後面的動詞該做什麼變化？

🔍 你先選選看

A: Any suggestions on how to improve my French?
B: I recommend **study / studying** in France for a year.

A: 你有什麼可以增進法語能力的建議嗎？
B: 我建議你去法國念個一年書。

Ans: studying

▶ recommend / suggest 有兩種不同用法：

recommend / suggest + 動名詞

We strongly recommend reporting the incident to the police.
我們強烈建議這件事要報警處理。

recommend / suggest + (that) + 人 + (should) + 原形 V

He recommended that I should buy a more powerful computer.
他建議我買台性能好一點的電腦。

▶ 請注意第二個用法，recommend / suggest 後接的是原形動詞，這是因為在表示「建議」的句型中，should 常被省略，以避免語氣太過強硬。

# 學西班牙文很簡單。

▶ 如果一個句子的主詞是一個動作,那該動作要轉變成什麼形態?

## 你先選選看

A: **Learning / Learn** Spanish is easy.
B: Well, at least it's easier than learning English.

A: 學西班牙文很簡單。
B: 這個嘛,至少比學英文簡單啦。

Ans: Learning

▶ 如果一個動作要擺句首當主詞,則要轉化為動名詞的形式(因為一個句子不能出現兩個動詞,除非有連接詞連接)。

Getting up early is really hard for me.
早起對我來說很難。

▶ 另一種作法是將動詞轉化成 to + 原形動詞,不過這種狀況極少出現在現代英語裡,通常是出現在一些俗諺中:

To err is human.
人都會犯錯。

To know him is to love him.
認識他就會喜歡他。

都幫你整理好,不要再問了!
主詞是動詞 → 將該動詞轉化成 Ving
或 to + V

# 你多常跟你老婆說你愛她？

▶ 「提及某事」，到底要說 mention sth. 還是 mention about sth.？

## 你先選選看

A: Did Bob tell you he got a promotion?
B: No. He didn't **mention about / mention** it.

A: 鮑伯有告訴你他升職了嗎？
B: 沒有。他都沒提。

Ans: mention

▶ 很多動詞後面其實不需加介系詞，但大家常常會誤加，例如 tell（告知）、discuss（討論）、contact（聯絡）等。

> How often do you <u>tell</u> your wife you love her?
> 你多常跟你老婆說你愛她？

> You should <u>discuss</u> the problem with your doctor.
> 你該跟你的醫生討論一下這個問題。

> I tried to <u>contact</u> him, but his phone is out of order.
> 我試著聯絡他，但他電話故障。

# 你明天要和我一起去逛街嗎？

▶ 很常在句子中看到 go + Ving 這種組合，請問這是什麼用法？

🔍 你先選選看

A: Would you like to go **shop / shopping** with me tomorrow?
B: Sure. I need to buy some new clothes.

A: 你明天要和我一起去逛街嗎？
B: 好啊。我得買幾件新衣服。

Ans: shopping

▶動詞 go 後面直接加動名詞，代表「從事某項活動」，日常對話中常聽到的 go shopping（去逛街）、go hiking（去健行）都是這種用法。

| I usually go swimming twice a week.
| 我通常一星期會去游泳兩次。

| Let's go dancing this Saturday.
| 我們這個星期六去跳舞吧。

更多例子：

go + {
fishing　釣魚
diving　浮潛
skiing　滑雪
sightseeing　遊覽
surfing　衝浪
bowling　打保齡球
parachuting　玩降落傘
}

I like to jog.

I like jogging.

I like to go jogging.

I like going jogging.
我喜歡慢跑。

# 動詞總複習
請選出適當的答案

1. Could you come _____ me move this bookcase?
   A. help
   B. helping
   C. to help
   D. helped

2. Are you used to _____ here yet?
   A. living
   B. live
   C. lived
   D. have lived

3. Have you considered _____ a smart phone?
   A. buy
   B. bought
   C. buying
   D. to buy

4. We were all _____ to hear about Ben's death.
   A. shocks
   B. shocked
   C. shock
   D. shocking

5. Simon regrets not _____ more when he was younger.
   A. traveling
   B. travel
   C. has traveled
   D. traveled

6. How much did it _____ you to fly in first class?

    A. take

    B. price

    C. spend

    D. cost

7. We _____ a lot more on food than we used to.

    A. cost

    B. shop

    C. spend

    D. buy

8. I expect you _____ your chores.

    A. did

    B. doing

    C. do

    D. to do

9. Rebecca had her nails _____ at the beauty salon.

    A. do

    B. done

    C. to do

    D. did

10. We suggest _____ at the airport two hours early.

    A. arrive

    B. arrival

    C. to arrive

    D. arriving

解答

1. A  2. A  3. C  4. B   5. A

6. D  7. C  8. D  9. B  10. D

# Chapter 5
# 時態
# Tenses

時態的惱人之處：

中文沒有時態，英文卻有十二種時態的分別，因此時態常常成為許多台灣人的罩門。

同樣都是描述過去的事，你分的出來過去式、過去完成式、過去完成進行式有什麼差別嗎？事件發生順序又是誰先誰後？
I finished my homework last night.
我昨天晚上寫完了作業。

I had finished my homework when you came last night.
昨天晚上你來的時候，我已經寫完我的作業。

When you came last night, I had been doing my homework for two hours.
昨天晚上你來的時候，我已經寫了兩個小時作業。

# 時態大哉問
## Questions About Using Tenses

時態有十二種，是要怎麼背啦？

學什麼語言都一樣，千萬不要被數字嚇到，名義上時態的確是有這麼多種，但是一理通、百理通，最重要、最常用的其實只有這五類：

▶ 現在簡單式（simple present）

一開始學時態的基本句都是先學這個時態，舉凡一般性的事實或真理、慣常的動作、不特別強調過去或未來的狀況下，都適用現在簡單式。在這種狀況下，第三人稱單數搭配的動詞加 s 或 es 即可。

I go jogging every morning.
我每天早上都去慢跑。
→ 每天都會做的事情。

The sun rises in the east.
太陽從東邊升起。
→ 亙古不變的事實。

如果要變成問句，助動詞用 do / does：

Does Mandy like cats?
蔓蒂喜歡貓嗎？

How do you like your steak?
你的牛排要幾分熟？

▶ 現在進行式（present progressive）

目前正在進行的動作或狀態，比較明顯的判斷字是 now。

Susan is writing a letter now.
蘇珊正在寫信。

▶ 過去簡單式（simple past）

過去發生且至今已完結的動作或狀態，通常過去式動詞大多加 ed，比較值得注意的是，通常這些句子會出現一些代表過去的字或片語，看到這些關鍵字就知道要用過去式。

ago　以前

this morning　今天早上

last week (night, Sunday)　上星期、昨晚、上週日

yesterday　昨天

the day before yesterday　前天

before　從前

in the past　在過去

just now　剛才

used to　以前

從這個時態開始就會運用到我們在「動詞」一章所提到的動詞變化，記得要牢記三態喔！

▶ 現在完成式（present perfect）

發生於過去，至今仍在進行中，句型為 have / has + p.p.，常出現的關鍵字有 for、since 等。

I have been to Korea several times.
我去過韓國幾次。

Aaron has lived here since he was eight.
艾倫從八歲就住在這裡。

▶ 未來式（future）

未來即將發生的事情，多使用到助動詞 will。

I will go to Sally's birthday party.
我會去莎麗的生日派對。

She won't marry you because she doesn't love you.
她不會嫁給你的，因為她不愛你。

當然，這些是最基本的五大時態，若要細分，組合可以是簡單式、進行式、完成式、完成進行式這四大類，每類又分過去、現在和未來，所以總共是十二種。

你上面提到的五大時態還好啊，到底難在哪？

這麼有自信？那我問問你過去進行式跟過去式有什麼不一樣？ gonna 是什麼意思，後面要接怎樣的動詞？在未來式中，什麼情況助動詞會用 would，什麼狀況用 will？ 這些眉眉角角確定你都會？如果答不出來，那就要趕快翻開本章，讓你看看時態到底哪裡有問題！

# { 蘇想去夏威夷很久了。 }

▶ 現在完成進行式適用於什麼狀況？

你先選選看

A: Should we invite Sue to go with us to Hawaii?
B: Sure. She's been **wanted / wanting** to go there for a long time.

A: 我們應該邀蘇跟我們一起去夏威夷嗎？
B: 好啊。她想去那裡很久了。

Ans: wanting

▶ 現在完成進行式是用在某事於過去發生，一直持續到現在還在進行。上面這則題目中，蘇「從以前到現在」都很想去夏威夷，所以應該要用現在完成進行式。

▶ 現在完成進行式一樣有分主動和被動語態，在題目中，want 是主動的動作，因此用「主詞 + have / has been Ving」的句型。如果當中的動作屬被動的話，則是用「主詞 + have / has been p.p.」。

She has been writing the report for two hours.
她已經寫那份報告寫了兩個小時。

She has written the report.
她已經把報告寫好了。

The bank **has been robbed**.
那間銀行被搶了。

Eric **has been offered** a scholarship.
艾瑞克被授予獎學金。

都幫你整理好，不要再問了！
主詞 + have / has been Ving / p.p.
→現在完成進行式

# 我畢業後想繼續升大學。

▶ I'd 是什麼的縮寫？
▶ 在未來式中，什麼狀況會用 would，什麼狀況會用 will ？

## 你先選選看

A: Are you going to college after you graduate?
B: **I'll / I'd** like to go, but I can't afford it.

A: 你畢業後要繼續上大學嗎？
B: 我想，但我負擔不起。

Ans: I'd

▶ I'd 是 I would 的縮寫，用來表示假設的狀況，當中帶有不確定的意味，通常可能性較小且，而 I'll 則是 I will 的縮寫，指的是未來確定會做的事。

I'd pick you up, but I have to work late.
我會去接你，但我得加班。

I'll pick you up at seven.
我會七點去接你。

▶ 在題目中，I'd like to... 是常見的固定用法，表示「我想要／我喜歡…」。

# { 我希望這場雨不要再下了。 }

▶ 要表明「對未來的期望」，助動詞要用哪一個？

🔍 你先選選看

A: I wish it **will / would** stop raining.
B: Me too. It's been raining for days.

A: 我希望這場雨不要再下了。
B: 我也希望。這雨已經下了好幾天了。

Ans: would

▶ 助動詞 would / could 與 wish 連用時，表示說話者「希望」某事將來發生，但該願望有可能不會實現。

I wish our son <u>would</u> get a job and move out.

I wish our son <u>could</u> get a job and move out.
我希望咱倆的兒子能夠找份工作然後搬出去。

▶ 這兩句的中文看來相去不遠，但內在的含義有些不同。第一句用助動詞 would，跟「個人意願」比較有關，例如他兒子可能是不想找工作所以還沒找到工作；第二句用助動詞 could，意思比較偏向「能力、環境」不允許，可能是學歷不夠，或是景氣不好，導致他沒工作。

💬 都幫你整理好，不要再問了！
I wish...would / could...

# {法蘭克已經看過那場展覽了。}

▶ 過去式和過去完成式的差別在哪？

🔍 你先選選看

A: Did Frank go with you to the exhibit?
B: No. He said he **had seen / see** it already.

A: 法蘭克有陪你去看展覽嗎？
B: 沒有。他說他已經看過了。

---

A: When did Frank see the exhibit?
B: He **went / had gone** to see it last week.
A: 法蘭克什麼時候去看那個展覽的？
B: 他上星期去的。

Ans: had seen, went

▶ 以上的問題是考考大家對英文過去時態的基本判斷。不過先別管文法公式了，先來看看以下這兩個例句有什麼差別：

> I went to Warner Village to see *Bride Wars* yesterday.
> 我昨天去華納威秀看了《新娘大作戰》。

> I asked Hank to come to the movie with me yesterday, but he told me he had seen it already.
> 我昨天問漢克要不要跟我去看電影，但是他說已經看過了。

▶ 有沒有發現，第一個句子講的是「昨天」的事，動詞用過去式 went 很合理；第二個句子則出現了 had + p.p. 的動詞形態，這就是「過去完成式」的用法。兩句話適用的狀況差在「動作發生的時間點」。

▶ 總括來說，過去式是跟「現在的時間」做先後比較；過去完成式是「兩個過去的時間」做先後比較。

▶ 更簡單的記法就是，在描述過去的句子中：

只出現一個動作→用 V-ed
出現兩個動作→較靠近現在的動作用 V-ed，更早的動作用 had + p.p.

> When I left the house, it had already started raining.
> 我出門的時候已經開始下雨。

> Ron had never studied French before he went to Paris.
> 榮恩在去巴黎前從沒學過法文。

都幫你整理好，不要再問了！

簡單過去式 S + V-ed

過去完成式 S + had + p.p.

# 你有去過太浩湖嗎？

▶ have gone 和 have been 的意思有何不同？

🔍 你先選選看

A: Do you know where Steven is?
B: I think he's **gone / been** to Tokyo on business.

A: 你知道史蒂芬在哪裡嗎？
B: 他好像去東京出差了。

---

A: Have you ever **gone / been** to Lake Tahoe before?
B: No, but I've always wanted to go.
A: 你有去過太浩湖嗎？
B: 沒有，但我一直很想去。

Ans: gone, been

▶ 上面這兩個題目中，第一題想表達的是「史蒂芬已經去了東京，並且現在還在那裡」，因此要選 has gone to；第二題則是想尋問對方是否有去過太浩湖，主要是指「過去的一段經歷」，所以要選 have been。

| Kevin <u>has gone to</u> lunch, and should be back in half an hour.
| 凱文去吃午餐了，應該一小時內會回來。

| We<u>'ve been to</u> Paris twice since we got married.
| 我們結婚後去過兩次巴黎。

**Where have you gone?**
你去哪裡了？
→ 對方還在那裡

**Where have you been?**
你去了哪裡？
→ 對方已經回來了

都幫你整理好，不要再問了！

have gone →強調「去某地、去做什麼」的這個動作，並且到現在還是維
　　　　　持該動作

have been →強調「曾經到過某地」的經歷

## 我的車昨晚被偷了。

如何用英文表達「被…」的狀態？

A: Why were you late to work?
B: My car was **stolen / stole** last night.

A: 你為什麼上班遲到？
B: 我車昨晚被偷了。

Ans: stolen

▶ 被動語態是由「be 動詞 + 過去分詞」組成。

People eat mushrooms in salads.
人們會把蘑菇放進沙拉中食用。

Mushrooms are eaten (by people) in salads.
蘑菇被放進沙拉中好讓人食用。

▶ 被動語態使用時機為「當描述物品或描述過程比描述主詞、動作還重要，或是主詞是不確定的、不重要的，或者是主詞是大家都知道的」的情況下。

Somebody has fed the dog.
有人餵了狗。
→ The dog has been fed.
狗被餵了。

George took these photos.
喬治拍了這些相片。
→ These photos were taken by George.
這些相片是喬治拍的。

▶ 在被動語態中，提到「動作者」時，要用 by，提到「工具」時，則用 with。

The sonnet was written <u>by</u> Shakespeare.
這首十四行詩是莎士比亞寫的。

The cake was cut <u>with</u> a knife.
蛋糕是用刀子切開的。

 都幫你整理好，不要再問了！

be + p.p. + by + 做動作者

be + p.p. + with + 工具

# 我今晚要去約會。

▶ 現在式和現在進行式的適用差別為何？

🔍 你先選選看

A: Why are you in such a hurry?
B: Because the movie **starts / is starting** in half an hour.

A: 你為什麼這麼趕？
B: 因為電影半小時後就要開始了。

---

A: Why are you all dressed up?
B: Because **I go / I'm going** on a date tonight.

A: 你幹嘛這麼盛裝打扮？
B: 因為我今晚要去約會。

Ans: starts, I'm going

▶ 現在式可以用在很多情況，以上題的例子來說，通常現在式是用在預定好，或是在常態下普遍會發生的動作：

My flight <u>leaves</u> at seven in the morning.
我的班機早上七點起飛。

A bus <u>comes</u> every 15 minutes.
公車每十五分鐘會來一班。

→ 以上兩句都只是陳述事實，不強調發生在過去還是未來，因此用現在式。

▶除強調「當下正在進行的動作」會用到現在進行式之外，如果是想表達「馬上會去做某事」，也可用現在進行式。

I'm meeting my friends at the mall at 2:00.
我兩點會在購物中心和我朋友碰頭。

I'm going grocery shopping later.
我晚點會去超市買東西。

多學一點，加深印象！

▶因為「馬上會去做」表示現在還沒做，因此在這種情況下，**be Ving** 也可以用未來式 **will** + 原形動詞替換。

# 我去倒垃圾的時候在下雨。

▶ 過去式和過去進行式不都是在講已經發生的事情嗎？該怎麼分呢？

🔍 你先選選看

A: You look terrible. Are you sick?
B: No, just tired. I **stayed up / was staying up** late studying every night last week.

A: 你氣色好差。你生病了嗎？
B: 沒有，我只是累了。我上星期每晚都熬夜唸書。

---

A: Is it raining now?
B: I'm not sure. It **rained / was raining** when I took out the trash.
A: 現在正在下雨嗎？
B: 不確定耶。我去倒垃圾的時候在下雨。

> Ans: stayed up, was raining

▶ 過去式很好判別，只要表示過去的狀態，或是過去經常發生的情況，都是用過去式。

| I <u>had</u> a cold the whole time I was in Tokyo.
| 我去東京的時候整趟都在感冒。

| When I was little, I always <u>watched</u> cartoons after school.
| 當我很小的時候，我放學都會看卡通。

▶ 當強調一件過去的事情「在過去的某時刻正在進行」，就用過去進行式，看看以下例子：

I was driving to work at eight this morning.
我今早八點的時候正在開車去上班。

▶ 在整個過去時段中，一件事已經發生且持續進行的當下，又發生另一件事，也會用到過去進行式。

I was taking a shower when you called.
你打來的時候我正在洗澡。

# 時態總複習

1. _____ love to go with you, but I already have plans.
   A. I
   B. I'd
   C. I'll
   D. I've

2. Are you gonna _____ your parents what happened?
   A. telling
   B. to tell
   C. will tell
   D. tell

3. The class _____ a reading assignment.
   A. was given
   B. gave
   C. was gave
   D. given

4. Ellen _____ her homework now.
   A. is done
   B. does
   C. do
   D. is doing

5. My mom and I often _____ on the phone.
   A. talking
   B. to talk
   C. talk
   D. talks

6. Have you _____ the project yet?

    A. finishing

    B. finish

    C. finished

    D. to finish

7. Rick has _____ to the bank, and should be back soon.

    A. gone

    B. been

    C. went

    D. go

8. I've been _____ for you for almost an hour.

    A. waited

    B. wait

    C. waiting

    D. have waited

9. Our dog _____ the mailman yesterday.

    A. bite

    B. bit

    C. bitten

    D. bites

10. If I'd _____ it was your birthday, I would've bought you a gift.

    A. knows

    B. known

    C. know

    D. knew

解答

1. B   2. D   3. A   4. D   5. C

6. C   7. A   8. C   9. B   10. B

153

# Chapter 6
# 假設語氣
# The subjective mood

討厭的假設語氣難在哪？

假設句分成有可能發生、不會發生的事件；而不會發生的事件又分成與現在事實相反、與過去事實相反…錯綜複雜，每考必掛！

中文要表達「假設」的語氣，只要加個「可能」、「或許」之類的關鍵字就好，完全不用顧慮時態問題，然而假設語氣卻跟時態綁在一起，難度倍增。

# 假設語氣大哉問
## Questions About Using the Subjective Mood

假設語氣就用 if 這個字表示就好了，有什麼難的？

不不不，if 所形成的假設語氣可歸成五種情況，而且每個情況都起碼會用到兩種時態，要非常注意 if 引導的子句要用什麼時態，非常困難！先給你個句子瞧瞧，自己翻翻看，感受一下假設語氣的邏輯吧！

> If Mary _____ to my birthday party, I _____ glad.
> 如果瑪麗來我的生日派對，我會很開心。

Step 1: 這是跟現在事實相反？跟過去事實相反？還是其他屬性的句子？

這句話既不是跟以前發生過的事情相反，也不是跟現在的事實相反，而是純粹表達一種條件，如果「瑪麗來派對」的這個條件具備了，我就會很開心。因此這只是一個「純條件的假設語氣」。

Step 2: if 所引導的子句要用什麼時態？

在以上這個例子中，if 子句表純條件，因此用現在式就可以了，而後面的句子指的是尚未發生的事情，因此用未來式。所以這題的答案是：

If Jane <u>comes</u> to my birthday party, I <u>will be</u> glad.

我知道假設語氣該注意哪些點了，但其他的假設語氣又有什麼規則呢？

假設語氣基本上可分為五種：

1. 純條件的假設語氣
2. 與現在事實相反的假設語氣
3. 與過去事實相反的假設語氣
4. 與未來狀況相反的假設語氣
5. 表示與真理相反的假設語氣

除了第五種比較特殊，其他四種都還滿常見的，有個很簡單的記憶法：

**純條件**→ if 子句用現在式

**與現在相反**→ if 子句用過去式

**與過去相反**→ if 子句用過去完成式

**與未來相反**→ if 子句用助動詞 should，主要子句用現在是或過去式助動詞

If you asked me to marry you, I would say yes without hesitation.
如果你（現在）跟我求婚，我會毫不考慮地答應。

If my mom had been there, I wouldn't have been bullied.
如果我媽（當時）在場，我就不會被欺負了。

If anything should happen to you, I would never forgive myself.
要是你（將來）有個三長兩短，我永遠也不會原諒我自己。

看出端倪了嗎？ if 所引導的子句，動詞形態都要「往前推一格」，與現在相反就用過去式，與過去相反就用過去完成式，很好記吧？

除了用 if 之外，我知道假設語氣也常用在「許願」，表達「希望某事發生」，該怎麼說？

有概念喔，知道 wish 和 hope 要用假設語氣。其原則與上述所提的一樣，都是「往前推一格」，但有一點很特別：

I wish he were here.
我希望他（現在）在這裡。

與現在事實相反，用過去式，但無論主詞是第幾人稱，be 動詞一律都要用 were。

其他還有更多關於假設語氣的眉眉角角，現在就趕快翻開後面的章節，好好把假設語氣給搞定吧！

# 如果你願意，我可以載你回家。

▶ 表「如果」的連接詞 if，後面用不同時態的意義有何不同？

🔍 你先選選看

A: If you **has come / come** to San Francisco, you can stay at my house.
B: Great! Thanks for the offer.

A: 如果你來舊金山，你可以住在我家。
B: 太好了！謝謝你的款待。

Ans: come

▶ 在上題中，if 子句表示的是「條件」，敘述的是一件有可能會發生的事，用現在簡單式：

If you like, I can give you a ride home.
如果你願意，我可以載你回家。

▶ 記得這個用法可別和「與現在事實不符」以及「與過去事實不符」的假設句混淆了：

If I were rich, I would live in a mansion.
如果我有錢，我就會去住豪宅。
→ 與現在事實不符

If we had arrived earlier, we could have bought tickets.
如果我們早點到，我們就買得到票了。
→ 與過去事實不符

# 如果我還年輕，我就會約她出去了。

▶ 與現在事實相反的假設語氣，be 動詞該作何變化？

你先選選看

A: The new receptionist is pretty, isn't she?
B: Yeah. If I **were / was** younger, I'd ask her out.

A: 那個新來的櫃檯小姐很漂亮對吧？
B: 對啊。如果我還年輕，我就會約她出去了。

Ans: were

▶ 以上題目是表達與現在事實相反的情況，一般都用過去式動詞，但遇到 be 動詞的話比較特別，配上 I 的話不是用 was，而是用 were。其中最常聽到例子就是 If I were you（如果我是你的話），大家都知道兩個人根本是不同的個體，所以這句話要表達的是一種永遠無法成真的假設語氣。不過在口語上，即便以文法來說不正確，但很多人都會用 was 而不說 were。

If I were you, I'd accept her apology.
如果我是你，我會接受她的道歉。

多學一點，加深印象！

▶ 與現在事實相反，主詞是 I 的時候，be 動詞要搭配 were。

# { 真希望我可以跟你一起去旅行。 }

▶ 用 wish 表達願望時，在時態上有什麼要注意的地方？

 你先選選看

> A: I wish I **were / was** going on the trip with you.
> B: So do I. I'll miss you while I'm gone.
>
> A: 真希望我可以跟你一起去旅行。
> B: 我也是。你不在的時候我會想你的。
>
> Ans: were

▶ 對過去和現在的事實用動詞 wish 提出假設時，代表「事與願違」的希望，後面常接用 that 引導的名詞子句，子句的動詞變化必須「往前推一格」，看以下的句子就知道：

I wish my wife <u>were</u> a better cook.
我希望我老婆的廚藝可以進步一點。

▶ 從這個例句中，說話者老婆的廚藝差強人意是「現在既存的事實」，所以子句的 be 動詞就往前推，用過去式，但切記在假設語氣中，要用 were 而不是用 was。

Monica wishes she <u>had been</u> with her parents when the accident happened.
莫尼卡真希望意外發生時，她和父母在一起。

▶ 這個例子中，莫尼卡父母發生意外是已發生的事，所以子句時態是用「過去完成式」。

💬 都幫你整理好，不要再問了！
對現況的願望 → 動詞用「過去式」，be 動詞一律用 were
wish (+that) + S. + were / Ved
對過去的願望 → 動詞用「過去完成式」
wish (+t hat) + S. + had + p.p

# 它會害我做惡夢。

▶ 對話中常聽到的 gonna 是什麼意思？

A: This movie is so scary!
B: Yeah. It's gonna **give / giving** me nightmares.

A: 這部電影好恐怖！
B: 對啊。它會害我做惡夢！

Ans: give

▶ 在口語英文中，be gonna 就是 be going to 的意思，表示未來的計畫，後方接原形動詞。

A: Are you gonna invite Kathy to your party?
你要約凱西去你的派對嗎？

B: No, 'cause she didn't invite me to hers.
不要，因為她辦派對時沒有邀我。

多學一點，加深印象！

▶ be going to 和 will 有時可以互換，表示「未來即將發生的事」，但若要細分，其實 be going to 比較偏向「依據外在狀況和環境而定的結果」，而 will 則偏向「由說話者主控的結果」。

The weather report says it's going to rain today.
氣象報告說今天會下雨。

I said I'd fix the sink, and I will.
我說了我會去修水槽，我就是會去。

161

# 你當初該用功點的。

如何用英文表達「早該…」？

## 你先選選看

A: I failed my history exam.
B: You **should / should've** studied harder.

A: 我歷史測驗沒過。
B: 你當初該用功一點的。

Ans: should've

▶ 在英文中，若要表示「早就該…」，就要用 should have + p.p.。這個用法通常帶有「沒做到某事，現在後悔當初沒做」的含意，屬於「與過去事實相反的假設語氣」。

He should've <u>stayed</u> in school and finished his degree.
你當初應該留在學校完成學業的。

▶ 若是要表達「當初不該…」 shouldn't have + p.p.

I <u>shouldn't have eaten</u> so much at the buffet.
我在自助餐不應該吃那麼多的。

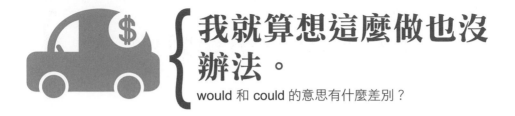

# 我就算想這麼做也沒辦法。

would 和 could 的意思有什麼差別？

你先選選看

A: Steve asked me out. Do you think I should say yes?
B: If I were you, I **wouldn't / couldn't** go out with him.

A: 史蒂夫約我出去。你覺得我應該答應嗎？
B: 如果我是你，我不會跟他出去。

A: Why don't you buy a new car?
B: I **wouldn't / couldn't** even if I wanted to. I don't have enough money.

A: 你幹嘛不買輛新車？
B: 我就算想這麼做也沒辦法。我沒有足夠的錢。

Ans: wouldn't, couldn't

▶ 在假設語氣的句子中，would 是表示該件事「會不會發生」，而 could 則是表示「有沒有可能發生」或「能不能這樣做」，也就是「發生這件事的條件充不充足」。

I would have dinner with you if didn't have to work late.
我如果不用加班的話，就會跟你吃晚餐了。

If you tossed the coin in the water it would sink.
如果你把硬幣丟進水裡，它就會沉下去。

I could lend you the money, but I'm not going to.
我是可以借錢給你，但我不會。

It could rain later, so you should take an umbrella.
晚點可能會下雨，所以你該把傘帶著。

If you <u>could</u> have lunch with any famous person, who <u>would</u> you choose?
如果你可以與隨便一個名人共進晚餐，你要跟誰？

▶ 如果是在「禮貌地請求對方做某事」，在這種情況下，用 would 或 could 開頭都可以，沒什麼差別。

Could you (please) tell me where the nearest MRT station is?
請問離這裡最近的捷運站在哪？

Would you (please) do me a favor?
可以請你幫個忙嗎？

Would you mind not smoking?
可以請你不要抽菸嗎？

Would you like to come to our house for dinner?
你想不想來我們家吃晚餐？

Would you like another piece of cake?
你還想再吃一片蛋糕嗎？

# 假設語氣總複習

請選出適當的答案

1. If you _____ me to leave, I will.

   A. told

   B. tell

   C. telling

   D. will tell

2. If I _____ you, I'd quit smoking.

   A. am

   B. was

   C. are

   D. were

3. If anyone calls, please _____ a message.

   A. be taking

   B. takes

   C. take

   D. to take

4. If you _____ me, I wouldn't have forgotten.

   A. had reminded

   B. remind

   C. reminded

   D. were going to remind

5. Jacob wishes that he _____ harder in school.

   A. studied

   B. has studied

   C. studies

   D. had studied

6. Colin _____ spent more time studying for the exam.

   A. should

   B. should've

   C. shouldn't

   D. couldn't

7. If you _____ breakfast, you'll just have more for lunch.

   A. didn't eat

   B. hadn't eaten

   C. don't eat

   D. won't eat

8. If he'd had the money, he _____ a house.

   A. would buy

   B. had bought

   C. would bought

   D. would've bought

9. If _____ late, I won't wait for you.

   A. you're

   B. you will be

   C. you'd

   D. you've

10. If I'd chosen a different career, I _____ rich.

   A. could be

   B. could've been

   C. should be

   D. will be

解答

1. B  2. D  3. C  4. A  5. D

6. B  7. C  8. D  9. A  10. B

# Chapter 7
# 名詞
# Nouns

名詞的狡猾之處：

名詞實在太多了，學也學不完。

名詞可不可數已經夠難分了，有時候不可數名詞還可以加 s，讓人很錯亂。

有時名詞會轉化成別的詞性，讓人搞不清楚到底是什麼詞。

# 名詞大哉問
## *Questions About Using Nouns*

### 名詞到底有幾類啊？

名詞可以按照不同屬性分為好幾種，其實也不需要一次全部記清，遇到的時候就知道了。大部分可分為可數名詞、不可數名詞、專有名詞、普通名詞、專有名詞、抽象名詞、物質名詞。

### 哪些名詞字首要大寫？我每次都搞不清楚！

這個問題雖看似基本，但很多人都還是常常忘記。通常專有名詞的字首都要大寫，常見的專有名詞有這些：

· 地名和國名：Taiwan, Japan, France...

· 人名：Mandy, Tom...

· 日期：Christmas, Chinese New Year, April...

· 學科：Korean、Sociology...

▶ 專有名詞前面通常不加 a, an, the 這些冠詞，也不能在後面加 s，但我還是有看過例外，這是什麼狀況？

> I'm afraid you dialed the wrong number. We don't have a Mr. White.
> 我想您恐怕是打錯電話了，我們這裡沒有姓懷特的先生。

> There are two Toms in our office.
> 我們辦公室有兩位叫湯姆的人。

當專有名詞被當成普通名詞的時候，就可以加冠詞或 s 囉。

▶ 有些名詞明明聽起來是複數，動詞卻用單數動詞？

你說的應該是集合動詞吧？集合動詞就是以群體當成同一單位的集合體，例如：

army　軍隊
band　樂團
club　社團
family　家庭
team　隊伍
audience　觀眾
crowd　人群
majority　大多數

以上這些名詞視為一個大單位的單數，因此常會搭配單數動詞，但若要強調它是「一群個體」時，則會用複數動詞。

有時候會有好幾個名詞串在一起，導致整個句子又臭又長，根本不知道整句是什麼意思，怎麼辦？

通常這種情況應該是碰上「複合名詞」了，也就是將兩個名詞拼在一起，變成一個字，用來當成形容詞，例如：

one-day trip
English-speaking person

也有把其中一個名詞假裝成形容詞，用來修飾後面的名詞，例如：

diamond ring
blood pressure

除了上述這些問題，還有更多細節都在後面我們幫你整理的重點裡，記得要好好讀，下次別再問了啊！

# { 我每天都喝兩杯咖啡。 }

▶ 有時候會看到不可數名詞後面卻加了 s，這是什麼意思？

## 你先選選看

A: What did you do today?
B: I bought some new **furniture / furnitures** for my apartment.

A: 你今天做了什麼？
B: 我替我的公寓買了新傢俱。

---

A: How much coffee do you drink?
B: I drink two **coffee / coffees** every day.

A: 你喝多少咖啡？
B: 我每天都喝兩杯咖啡。

Ans: furniture, coffees

▶ 首先，可數名詞若為複數則要加 s，但不可數名詞則不能加，例如以下這些：
furniture　傢俱
work　工作
luggage　行李
advice　建議
information　資訊
wealth　財富
luck　好運

▶ 記得，可數名詞和不可數名詞前面用的形容詞也不同：

I brought <u>lots of</u> luggage with me.
我帶了很多行李。

I brought <u>three</u> suitcases on my trip.
我在這趟旅途中買了三個公事包。

How <u>much</u> butter did you put in the cookies?
你在餅乾裡放了多少奶油？

I wish you <u>lots of</u> luck.
祝你好運滿滿。

After the snowstorm, the ground was covered with snow.
暴風雪過後，地上佈滿冰雪。

▶ 按照一般原則，不可數名詞不能加 s，但若是人們習慣以容器盛裝的不可數名詞，在口語中也會加上 s，代表「有幾個容器單位」，有時還可代表「種類」。

I'd like <u>two vegetable soups</u> to go.
我要外帶兩碗蔬菜湯。
→ two 指的是容器「兩碗」，所以不可數的 soup 加 s 變複數。

How <u>many sugars</u> do you want in your tea?
你的茶要加多少糖？
→ 這裡的單位是「顆」、「包」等裝糖的容器。

France produces the finest <u>wines</u> in the world.
法國出產全球最棒的酒。
→ 這裡的 wines 指的是「不同種類的酒」。

## 大家都會去。

▶ everybody 和 everyone 指的是很多人，動詞該用複數嗎？

你先選選看

A: Is your whole family going on the trip?
B: Yes. Everybody **is / are** going.

A: 你全家都要一起出遊嗎？
B: 對啊。大家都要去。

Ans: is

▶ 千萬不要以為 everyone 或 everybody 的意思是「每個人」所以要用複數的 be 動詞 are，其實在這裡要把 everyone 看成一個單數的整體，如果後面要接動詞的話，也別忘了要把動詞後面加上 s / es。

Every one of the students is present.
每一位同學都出席了。

▶ 在上面的例句中，主詞是 every one，意為「每一個」，要視為單數，因此動詞也要用單數形態。

都幫你整理好，不要再問了！
everyone、everybody → 視作單數

# 我覺得你我不該再見面了。

▶ 當主格涉及兩個以上的代名詞，例如 you、she、I，連用時順序為何？

## 你先選選看

A: I don't think **I and you / you and I** should see each other anymore.
B: Are you breaking up with me?

A: 我認為你我不該再見面了。
B: 你是要跟我分手嗎？

Ans: you and I

▶ you、I、he / she、they…等稱之為代名詞（pronoun），在對話中當作主格，當代名詞一起連用時，它們的順序有一定的排列，並會因為單數、複數的不同，排列也隨之不同。

▶ 單數時的排列為：you, he / she and I

> You, she and I are invited to the party this Saturday night.
> 你、她還有我受邀參加這個星期六晚上的派對。

▶ 複數時的排列為：we, you and they

> We and you should get together sometime.
> 我們和你們應該找個時間聚一聚。

# 這是蔬菜湯。

▶ 有時候會看到兩個名詞接連出現,這樣在文法上是正確的嗎?

🔍 你先選選看

A: Does the soup have vegetables in it?
B: Yes. It's **vegetable / vegetables** soup.

A: 湯裡有蔬菜嗎?
B: 有。這是蔬菜湯。

A: Do you have any children?
B: Yes. I have a seven-**year / years**-old daughter.

A: 你有小孩嗎?
B: 有。我有個七歲的女兒。

Ans: vegetable, year

▶ 是的,你沒看錯,這樣的寫法不是錯誤的喔!有時候的確會把名詞轉化成形容詞來用,例如:

Emma has a <u>flower garden</u> in her backyard.
愛瑪的後院有個花圃。

Which <u>shoe store</u> do you buy your shoes at?
你都去哪家鞋店買鞋?

We're going on a <u>five-day</u> trip to Seoul.
我們要去首爾旅行五天。

It's a <u>nine-mile</u> hike to the top of the mountain.
爬上山頂要九哩的路程。

## {我晚餐吃牛排和馬鈴薯。}

▶ 有些名詞的複數形是加 es 而不是 s，有什麼規則嗎？

🔍 你先選選看

A: What are we having for dinner?
B: Steak and **potatos / potatoes**.

A: 你晚餐吃什麼？
B: 牛排和馬鈴薯。

Ans: potatoes

▶ potato 的複數形是要加上 es，其他還有許多以 o 結尾的字複數形也要加上 es，如 tomatoes…等。但並不是適用於所有 o 結尾的字，如 piano、photo 等是直接在字尾加上 s。

> War heroes are honored on Memorial Day.
> 戰時的英雄都在紀念日

> How many kilos do you weigh?
> 你幾公斤？

多學一點，加深印象！

▶ 其他特殊的複數變化：

f 或 fe 結尾的名詞，將 f 改為 v，再加 es：

> The ground was covered with fallen <u>leaves</u>.
> 地上鋪滿了落葉。

字尾是子音 + y，去 y 加 ies：

> Did your parents read you <u>stories</u> when you were little?
> 你小時候爸媽有沒有念故事書給你聽？

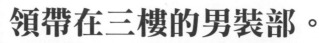

# 領帶在三樓的男裝部。

▶ 所有格的's 很惱人,不知道什麼時候該用's,什麼時候要用 s'。

## 你先選選看

A: When is the **girl's / girls'** birthday?
B: Her birthday is April 16, 1998.

A: 那個女孩的生日是何時?
B: 她生日是一九九八年四月十六日。

---

A: Can you tell me where the ties are?
B: They're in the **men's / mens'** department on the third floor.

A: 可以麻煩你告訴我領帶在哪裡嗎?
B: 在三樓的男裝部。

Ans: girl's, men's

▶ 這的確是個出錯率很高的問題,所有格的一撇該撇在哪裡,主要是看該名詞為單數或複數而定,單數名詞的所有格就是「名詞's」,但如果該名詞已經是 s 結尾了,那麼一撇就撇在最後即可:

Sally's grades are improving this semester.
沙莉這學期的成績有在進步。

Is that James' (James's) car parked over there?
停在那裡的那輛是詹姆士的車嗎?

第二種 James's 的寫法也是正確的,有時候在報章雜誌會看到,英國人也滿常這樣寫。

▶複數的名詞，則寫成「名詞 s'」，但若該名詞本身即為複數，那麼要寫成「名詞's」。

The couple sent their daughter to a girls' school.
那對夫婦送他們的女兒去讀女校。

The author mostly writes children's books.
那那位作家大部分寫的都是童書。

# 名詞總複習

請選出適當的答案

1. How _____ questions did you get wrong on the test?

    A. much

    B. large

    C. many

    D. huge

2. I drank too _____ wine last night.

    A. much

    B. large

    C. many

    D. huge

3. You don't know my name, _____ ?

    A. don't you

    B. aren't you

    C. do you

    D. shall you

4. _____ all have blue eyes.

    A. You, she and I

    B. I, you and she

    C. You, I and she

    D. She, you and I

5. She learned how to _____ from her father.

    A. play a piano

    B. play the piano

    C. play piano

    D. play one piano

6. _____ everyone have a textbook?

A. Do

B. Does

C. Is

D. Are

7. Will the company be hiring new _____ soon?

A. worker

B. employee

C. staffs

D. staff

8. I like to _____ on the weekend.

A. play tennis

B. play the tennis

C. play a tennis

D. play at tennis

9. The family _____ lived here for at least 10 years.

A. have

B. has

C. were

D. used to

10. _____ can meet at the café

A. They, you and we

B. We, you and they

C. You, we, and they

D. You, they and we

解答

1. C   2. A   3. C   4. A    5. B

6. B   7. D   8. A   9. B   10. D

# Chapter 8
# 子句
# Clauses

子句的惱人之處：

獨立子句和附屬子句明明長得很像，真不知道為什麼一個要叫「獨立」、一個要叫「附屬」？你會分辨嗎？
Cindy is sleeping. → 獨立子句
I think that Cindy is sleeping. → 以 that 開頭的附屬子句

以 who / what / which / where 等字開頭的名詞子句，主詞動詞每次都放錯！畢竟中文裡可沒類似的規則。看看以下例子就知道了：

A：Where is he ？
　　他在哪裡？
 B：I don't know where is he. (X)
　　I don't know where he is. (O)
　　我不知道他在哪裡。

# 子句大哉問
## *Questions for Using clauses*

### 子句跟句子差在哪裡？有子句也會有「母句」嗎？

不懂沒關係，懂得問才會學得快！很多文法用語大家小時候聽老師講到爛掉，但是如果對英文沒感覺，很容易想半天也想不通。其實文法是用來幫助大家歸納，學得更有效率，看到新名詞別害怕，看看下面例子包準你馬上驚呼：這也太簡單了吧～

句子（sentence）就是在句點或是其他停頓記號前的那一長串話。在英文裡，句子的開頭要大寫，如果中間用 and 之類的連接詞，整串還是算一個句子喔。

> The bad weather ruined our picnic.
> 壞天氣讓我們的野餐泡湯了。

這是一個有主詞動詞受詞的標準句子。

> I was born in the U.S. but I grew up in France.
> 我在美國出生，但在法國長大。

這也是一個句子，只是中間有連接詞。

子句（clause）是句子裡的小單位，只要有主詞動詞就自成一個子句。有些子句可以單獨存在，叫作獨立子句（main clause），有些子句因為意思不完整，需要依附在其他子句後，叫作附屬子句（subordinate clause）。獨立子句也可以叫「主句」，但母句可就沒聽過囉。

獨立子句 ↗
The party was great and we had a wonderful time!
獨立子句 ↙

派對很棒，我們玩得很開心。用 and 連接的兩個子句意思都很完整，都是獨立子句。

獨立子句 ↗
I need an umbrella because it is raining.
附屬子句 ↙

我需要一把傘，因為現在在下雨。句子講到前面就說完了，原因只是補充說明，如果光講因為在下雨會不清楚，只會讓人想問：「啊所以勒」

### 子句好像分好多種，到底要從何學起？

你有聽過名詞子句、形容詞子句、關係子句、副詞子句嗎？沒聽過的話也沒關係，不要被這些看似嚇人的術語打敗了，如果換成以下句型，說不定你早就會講了喔。

▶ 名詞子句

她不知道他去哪裡？ <u>She doesn't know where he went?</u>

他去哪裡用英文說應該是 Where did he go? 可是這裡是當成不知道的「事」，屬於一個附屬的名詞子句，也是間接問句。有

發現用 where 開頭的這個子句助動詞拿掉了嗎，what、when、who…等詞開頭的疑問句也要比照辦理，be 動詞也不必放到主詞前面。

I heard that you are getting married!
我聽說你要結婚了！

聽說的事情放在 that 後面，也是一個附屬的名詞子句。口語上常將 that 省略，沒聽到 that 可別大驚小怪。

Can you tell me if this bus goes to the airport?
你可以告訴我這班車有到機場嗎？

如果附屬子句是個 yes 或 no 的問句，疑問詞就要用 whether 或是 if。若要強調語氣，可在句末或是 whether 後加上 or not，if 後則不可加 or not。

▶ 形容詞子句

I like the dress that you are wearing.
我喜歡你穿的這件洋裝。

眼睛比較利的讀者應該看得出來，that 不是關係代名詞嗎？完全正確！後面的句子是一個附屬的關係子句，也有另一個名字叫形容詞子句，用來表示洋裝的性質，具有形容詞的功能。

▶ 副詞子句

亞當小的時候，每週都上教堂 When Adam was young, he used to go to Church every Sunday.

就像「因為」一定要配「所以」，好多數不清的連接詞，都像跟屁蟲一樣黏著主要子句，像表示條件的 unless（除非）；表示對比的 although（雖然）；表示時間的 since（自從）等等，它們帶的附屬子句是副詞子句，為主要子句加上了一個狀態。

說了這麼多，子句要怎麼用才會比較順？

如果每次跟外國人聊天都支支吾吾，講一個句子三五個字就結束了，不如試試用子句加長法做練習。用 I don't know 之類的句子當基礎，後面加 that 表達一件事情。例如：「我不知道誰是對的」、「我不知道哪條路才是往火車站的路」、慢慢再加上副詞子句或形容詞子句，偶爾也換換時態：「我不知道如果有一天我生病了，誰要來照顧我」、「我不知道為什麼我之前送你的東西你都不喜歡」，儘管天馬行空地把條件一一加長，試著讓句子更有深度，同時也練習到動詞擺放的位置、時態，講久了自然就會脫離萬年不變的 I don't know，英文也就更上一層樓囉。

# 你人真好，還來看我。

▶ 句型「It's nice of + 人」是什麼意思？

🔍 你先選選看

A: It's nice **of / that** you came to visit.
B: I'm glad I came.

A: 你人真好，還來看我。
B: 我很高興我來了。

Ans: that

▶ 這是說「某人（做某事），人真好」的句型，若是要用子句形式表達

It's nice of you to help me with my project.
你幫我做這個專案，人真好。

▶ 要是要用子句的形式表達，則用 that 連接：

It's nice that your boss gave you the day off.
你老闆真好，讓你放一天假。

 都幫你整理好，不要再問了！
It's nice of sb. ＋ to V
It's nice that ＋ 子句

# 你會來晚宴對吧？

附加問句的規則是什麼？

🔍 你先選選看

A: You're coming to the dinner party, **aren't / are** you?
B: I can't. I have to work late.

A: 你會來晚宴對吧？
B: 我無法。我要加班。

| Ans: aren't |

▶ 在直述句句尾後接的簡短問句稱為附加問句，如前面是肯定句，則需用否定的問句；反之如直述句有否定的意思，問句則需使用肯定。

| You ate the last piece of pie, didn't you?
| 你把最後一片派吃掉了，對吧？

| The coffee isn't very good, is it?
| 這咖啡不好喝，對吧？

▶ 要特別注意是以 Let's 開頭的直述句，不論肯定或否定附加問句都用 shall we?

| Let's get started, shall we?
| 我們開始好嗎？

 都幫你整理好，不要再問了！
肯定句→搭配否定附加問句
否定句→搭配肯定附加問句
Let's 開頭直述句→ shall 開頭的附加問句

# 你打來的時候我一定是睡著了。

▶ while 和 when 的意思有何不同？

🔍 你先選選看

A: Why didn't you answer the phone?
B: I must have been asleep **while / when** you called.

A: 你幹嘛不接電話。
B: 你打來的時候我一定是睡著了。

Ans: when

▶ 有時候 when 和 while 可以互換，但若要細分，when 後面通常會接持續時間較短的動作：

We were sitting in the living room watching TV when the power went off.
停電的時候我們正坐在客廳看電視。

▶ when 也可用在兩個在短時間內連續發生的的動作，或是純粹敘述簡單的事實：

When the teacher entered the classroom, all the students stopped talking.
當老師進教室時，所有學生都停止說話。

When I was a kid, I loved to read adventure stories.
當我還小的時候，我很愛看冒險故事。

▶ 在持續時間較長的動作中所發生的某個事件，或是兩動作同時進行，通常會用 while 表示：

Mike called for you while you were in the shower.
麥可在你洗澡時有打電話來。

I chopped the onions while Sally grated the cheese.
我一邊切洋蔥，莎利一邊磨起司。

▶ 把否定詞放句首的否定句，主詞和動詞的順序為何？

🔍 你先選選看

A: Never **have I / I have** been so insulted!
B: He really should apologize for saying those things to you.

A: 我從沒感到如此受辱！
B: 他真該為了對妳說那些話而道歉。

Ans: have I

▶ 當否定詞放句首時，主詞和動詞要倒裝，用意在強調「否定」的語氣：

Seldom had Allen seen anything stranger.
艾倫很少看到如此奇怪的事物。

Rarely have I seen such a beautiful sight.
我很少看到這麼美的景色。

Not only was the food delicious, but the prices were also cheap.
不只食物很好吃，價格也很實惠。

Under no circumstances is parking allowed here.
這裡絕不准停車。

# 我不確定他在哪裡工作。

▶ 間接問句或答句的句構是什麼？

🔍 你先選選看

A: Has Kevin found a job yet?
B: Yes, but I'm not sure where **he is / is he** working.

A: 凱文找到工作了沒？
B: 找到啦，不過我不確定他在哪裡工作。

Ans: he is

▶ 使用間接問句或答句時，要恢復成「直述句」的句構，也就是 S +V

現在進行式

| 直述句 → They are arguing.
          他們在爭吵。

| 疑問句 → What are they arguing about?
          他們在吵些什麼？

| 間接答句 → I don't know what they are arguing about.
            我不知道他們在吵什麼。

一般未來式

| 直述句 → The train will arrive at ten.
          火車十點會到。

| 疑問句 → When will the train arrive?
          火車幾點會到？

間接答句 → I'm not sure when the train will arrive.
我不知道火車幾點會到。

## 現在完成式

直述句 → They have been married for five years.
他們已經結婚五年了。

疑問句 → How long have they been married?
他們結婚多久了？

間接答句 → I don't remember how long they have been married.
我不記得他們結婚多久了。

## 一般過去式

直述句 → I decided to become a nurse.
我決定要當護士。

疑問句 → When did you decide to become a nurse?
你何時決定要當護士。

間接答句 → I forget when I decided to become a nurse.
我已經忘了我何時決定要當護士。

# { 球賽無論晴雨都會舉行。 }

▶ whether 和 if 的用法有何差別？

▶ whether 和 if 都有「是否」的意思，但用法稍有不同。whether...or not 可以寫成 whether or not：

Whether you want to or not, you must purchase auto insurance.

= Whether or not you want to, you must purchase auto insurance.
不管你想不想，你都得買車保。

▶ if...or not 則不能寫成 if or not：

I don't care if Christine likes me or not. (O)

I don't care if or not Christine likes me. (X)
我不在乎克麗絲汀喜不喜歡我。

# 那部電影真難看。

▶ 英文的感嘆語氣要怎麼表達？

🔍 你先選選看

A: **What / How** awful that movie was!
B: I know. It was really bad.

A: 那部電影真難看。
B: 我知道。真的很爛。

Ans: How

▶ 感嘆句有兩種，一種以 what 開頭，後面必須要加上名詞；一種是以 how 開頭，後面必須要加上形容詞或副詞。

名詞
What a clever girl you are!
妳真是個聰明的女孩！

形容詞
How beautiful you are!
你真美麗！

副詞
How fast he runs!
他跑得好快！

 都幫你整理好，不要再問了！
What + 名詞
How + 形容詞

# 子句總複習

1. It's nice _____ you to drive me to the airport.
   A. to
   B. for
   C. that
   D. of

2. Let's keep this a secret, _____?
   A. will we
   B. shall we
   C. should we
   D. do we

3. Sherry didn't pay attention to _____ the teacher was saying.
   A. that
   B. which
   C. what
   D. who

4. Do you know why _____ her job?
   A. she is quitting
   B. is she quitting
   C. she quits
   D. does she quit

5. Lisa wants to be a doctor _____ she grows up.
   A. while
   B. when
   C. as
   D. during

6. Kevin broke his leg _____ he was skiing.

   A. what

   B. when

   C. where

   D. while

7. Seldom _____ won so many gold medals.

   A. anyone has

   B. has anyone

   C. someone had

   D. he would

8. I forget _____ bought this scarf.

   A. where I did

   B. where did I

   C. where I

   D. where had I

9. _____ beautiful your necklace is!

   A. Very

   B. How

   C. So

   D. What

10. _____ a lovely day it is!

   A. Such

   B. Really

   C. How

   D. What

解答

1. D　2. B　3. C　4. A　　5. B

6. D　7. B　8. C　9. B　10. D

# Chapter 9
# 連接詞
# *Conjunction*

連接詞的惱人之處

連接詞不就 and 或 or，跟中文的「和」、「或」一樣簡單，哪有什麼惱人之處？如果你這麼想，可就大錯特錯了！連接詞可是分成四種，每一種都有要特別注意的地方，看完這章你就知道！例如以下

例句：
Not only my friends but also my sister likes it.
為什麼要用 likes 而不是 like？

偷偷告訴你，連接詞最惱人的地方叫做「平行結構」，也就是連接詞前後要名詞配名詞、形容詞配形容詞，講求門當戶對，很多人都忽略了這一點噢！你知道下面的句子錯在哪嗎？
What I like about him is his generosity, kindness and humorous.

# 連接詞大哉問
## *Questions About Using Conjunctions*

> 我知道什麼是連接詞，就是字跟字連在一起的詞對吧！

先生小姐啊，你說的是像 part-time 或是 five-year-old 這種把好幾個字連在一起的複合形容詞嗎？大錯特錯！雖然這些字中間的線叫做連字號，但跟連接詞一點關係也沒有！（順便教大家，連字號的英文叫做 hyphen，而不是一直被講錯的 dash，但時間寶貴，有空再好好說明）

連接詞顧名思義就是將字或句子連在一起的詞，最常見的連接詞例如 and、or、but... 等字，舉個例子來說：

> He is tall, rich and handsome.
> 大驚！這不是傳說中的高富帥嗎？快點把握啊。

▶ 連接詞如果不連接相同詞性，而隨便亂連一通，小心句子天下大亂！

連接詞使用時一定要注意，無論是連接兩個、三個或是多個詞組，前後的詞性一定要一致，名詞配名詞；形容詞配形容詞；子句配子句，不然就會讓人鴨子聽雷。

### 名詞配名詞

> Do you want some coffee or tea?
> 你想要喝點咖啡或是茶嗎？

### 動詞配動詞

> My little brother likes to sing and dance
> 我弟弟喜歡唱歌跳舞。

### 子句配子句

> It's a beautiful car but I can't afford it.
> 這輛車很漂亮，但我買不起。

這句話 but 的前面都有完整的主詞動詞受詞，所以 but 在此連接的是兩個子句

▶ 睜大雙眼，認出連接詞和它的祖宗十八代

因為連接詞有前後詞性須一致的特性，所以在句子中把全家人一起揪出來，就會比較容易判斷後面要加的字動詞時態之類的問題囉。但是先來學學有哪幾類連接詞吧：

對等連接詞：and、but、nor、or、yet、so

> Do you want to go out and watch a movie or stay home?
> 你想出去看場電影，還是待在家裡？

配對連接詞：not only...but (also)、neither...nor、either...or、whether...or、both...and

> The boy can neither read nor write.
> 那個男孩既不會閱讀也不會寫字。

從屬連接詞：although、because、before、if、than、until、when、while…這

類的連接詞有非常多，依照意思可分成時間、地點、原因、條件等不同類別，通常會跟著一個次要的子句出現，接在主要子句後面

I'll call you <u>when</u> I get back to the office.
我回到辦公室的時候會回電給你。

連接副詞：finally、then、for example、so、therefore、however、nevertheless…很多時候這些副詞也可以當連接詞使用，並且跟從屬連接詞一樣，依照意思分成不同類別

Kevin went to the department store; <u>but</u>, he didn't buy anything.
凱文去了百貨公司，但是他沒買任何東西。

## 配對連接詞的特殊文法

很奇怪，簡單的東西一定不如想像中那麼容易，或者該說老師就愛考那些稀奇古怪的文法，所以要學一定要一次搞清楚哩～

neither...nor、either...or 或 not only...but 夾著主詞時，動詞變化以最靠近的主詞決定

Neither Henry nor I <u>live</u> in Taipei.
我和亨利都不住在台北。

咦，好奇怪，這裡的 live 到底是單數還是複數？英文裡是任兩者之一，所以是單數，但動詞的變化是以最靠近的 I 來決定，超容易錯，眼睛最好張大點。

not only 開頭的句子，因為否定詞在句首，所以 be 動詞要倒裝放到主詞前面，普通動詞則要加上助動詞

Not only does he play tennis, but he also plays basketball.
他不僅會打網球，還會打籃球。

注意到了嗎，主詞的前面加了助動詞 does，是個確確實實的倒裝句喔！

# 我寧願在家吃。

 would rather 後面的動詞該用什麼形態？

## 你先選選看

A: Do you want to eat out tonight?
B: Actually, I'd rather **have / had** dinner at home.

A: 你今晚想出去外面吃嗎？
B: 其實我寧願在家吃。

Ans: have

▶ would rather 表示「寧願」的意思。I would 常會縮寫為 I'd：

I'd rather take the train.
我寧願坐火車。

▶「寧願…，而不…」則是 would rather...than...，其後要接原形動詞。

He'd rather read than watch TV.
他寧願看書也不要看電視。

▶ 使用過去式時，句型為 would rather have + 過去分詞

I'd rather have had tea than coffee.
我寧願當初點茶而不是咖啡。

都幫你整理好，不要再問了！
would rather + 原形動詞 + than + 原形動詞
would rather have + 過去分詞

# 儘管她曾對他不忠，他還是愛著她。

▶ despite 和 regardless 都是「儘管」，用法上有什麼不同？

🔍 你先選選看

A: Is Roger going to leave his wife?
B: No. He still loves her, **despite / regardless** the fact that she cheated on him.

A: 羅傑會離開他太太嗎？
B: 不會。儘管她曾對他不忠，他還是愛著她。

Ans: despite

▶ regardless 是「副詞」，解釋為「不顧一切地，不管怎樣」，可放於句尾或句首，但置於句首時，後面必須加上逗號，視同一種轉折語的用法。

▶ Regardless, S + V...　不管怎樣、雖然如此

The weather continued to worsen. Regardless, the climbers continued their ascent.
天氣持續惡化，不過登山者還是繼續往上爬。

▶ S + V... regardless.　不顧一切去做某事

Gary knew the milk was past its expiration date, but he drank it regardless.
蓋瑞明知牛奶過期，還是把它喝掉。

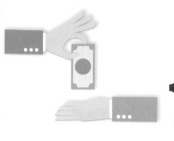

# 儘管我薪水很高，但我入不敷出。

▶ even 和 even if，以及 even though 有什麼不同？

A: Are you still going to the beach tomorrow? It's supposed to rain.
B: Yeah. I'm gonna go **even / even if** it rains.

A: 明天你還是要去海邊嗎？應該會下雨。
B: 我會去。就算下雨我也要去。

---

A: Why are you in debt? You have a good salary.
B: **Even if / Even though** I have a good salary, I spend more than I make.

A: 你為什麼會負債？你薪水很高耶。
B: 儘管我薪水很高，但我入不敷出。

> Ans: even if, Even though

▶ even 的意思是「甚至，連」，作用是加強語氣，為副詞：

| He always wears a sweater, even when it's hot.
| 他總是穿毛衣，連天氣很熱也是一樣。

| The meat tastes so bad even the dog won't eat it.
| 這肉超難吃，連狗都不吃。

▶ even if 意為「即使」，用於假設的情境，even though 則是用在實際發生的狀況，等於 although。

| Even if we leave right now, we'll still be late.
| 就算我們現在離開，還是會遲到。
| → 我們現在沒有要離開

# { 他不只忘了我的生日，還拒絕向我道歉。 }

not only...but also... 是什麼意思？該怎麼運用？

🔍 你先選選看

A: Why are you so mad at Karen?
B: She not only forgot my birthday **but / and** also refused to apologize.

A: 你為什麼這麼氣凱倫？
B: 她不只忘了我的生日，還拒絕向我道歉。

Ans: but

▶ but 通常用來連接兩個意義相反的字詞，或不合一般邏輯的因果：

| Alex is a smart boy, but he's very lazy.
艾利克斯是個聰明的男孩，但是他非常懶。

▶ not only A but (...) also B 除了 A，還有 B

| The car is not only affordable but also fun to drive.
這部車不但可以負擔得起，而且開起來也滿好玩的。

再多學一點，加深印象

▶ 除了 but，另外還有個字 yet 意思也與 but 差不多，都是用來連接前後不一致、不搭調的事情，中文常常可翻成「卻」。

| My room is small yet cozy.
我的房間雖小，但卻很舒適。

# {我想養一隻貓或狗。}

▶ either 和 both 後搭配的連接詞

🔍 你先選選看

A: What kind of pet would you like to have?
B: I'd like to have either a cat **and / or** a dog.

A: 你想要養哪種寵物？
B: 我想養貓或狗。

Ans: or

▶ either A or B　A 或 B 兩者之一

You can have <u>either</u> coffee <u>or</u> tea with your set meal.
你的套餐可以搭配咖啡或茶。

▶ both A and B　兩者都

Kevin played <u>both</u> baseball <u>and</u> football in high school.
凱文高中時有打棒球，也有踢美式足球。

▶ 表「兩者都不」的話，可以用 neither...nor... 這個片語，neither 本身即有否定之意：

Rebecca is <u>neither</u> a wife <u>nor</u> a mother.
蘿貝卡既不是人妻，也不是媽媽。

 都幫你整理好，不要再問了！
either...or... → 肯定
neither...nor... → 否定

{ 你寫完功課才能出去玩。 }

▷ until 和 unless 的意思和用法有何差別？

## 你先選選看

A: Can I go out and play now, Mom?
B: No. You can't go out **until / unless** you finish your homework.

A: 媽，我可以出去外玩嗎？
B: 不行，除非你寫完功課才能出去。

A: How late did you stay out last night?
B: I was out **until / unless** four in the morning

A: 你昨天在外面待到多晚？
B: 我在外面待到凌晨四點。

Ans: unless / until, until

▷ unless 和 until 都可當連接詞，unless 意為「如果不，除非」，而 until 則為「直到…時，到…為止」的意思，有時兩者意思可互通：

I'll stay here until it starts raining.
I'll stay here unless it starts raining.
我會一直待在這裡，除非開始下雨。

▷ 但是 until 可當作介系詞，unless 則不能：

I'll be working here until the end of the month. (O)
I'll be working here unless the end of the month. (X)
我會在這裡工作到本月底。

# 連接詞總複習

請選出適當的選項

1. The set meal comes with either soup _____ salad.
   A. no
   B. and
   C. or
   D. with

2. I'm a little tired, so I'd rather _____ home and rest.
   A. stayed
   B. staying
   C. to stay
   D. stay

3. Because it was a holiday, _____ the banks were closed.
   A. that all
   B. all
   C. so all
   D. and all

4. We enjoyed our trip to Florida _____ the bad weather.
   A. regardless
   B. although
   C. in spite
   D. despite

5. I failed the exam _____ I studied really hard.
   A. even though
   B. even
   C. even if
   D. if even

6. David speaks not only English _____ German.

    A. and also

    B. but also

    C. also

    D. or also

7. The dish contains _____ meat nor eggs.

    A. not

    B. either

    C. neither

    D. both

8. Even if you pass the final exam, you'll fail the course _____.

    A. regardless

    B. despite

    C. regardless of

    D. in spite

9. I wouldn't eat at that restaurant _____ it were free.

    A. even

    B. although

    C. even if

    D. even though

10. Neither Alex nor his brother _____ married.

    A. are

    B. is

    C. have

    D. were

解答
1. C   2. D   3. B   4. D   5. A
6. B   7. C   8. A   9. C   10. B

# *Chapter 10*
# 關係代名詞
# *Relative Pronouns*

「限定」、「非限定」，國高中時都聽到爛了，到現在還是搞不清楚哪時候要加逗號、哪時候不能加逗號…。

有時候 that／who／whom 可以互相替換，有時候又好像不行，不知道該怎麼分辨。

The guy that／who／whom we met just now is my ex.
以上情況，that／who／whom 都可以（但 whom 的用法越來越少見了）。

He is the guy that I told you about.　（○）
He is the guy about whom I told you.　（○）
He is the guy about who I told you.　（×）
在這裡，不能用 about who 替換 about whom，為什麼呢？

# 關係代名詞大哉問
## Questions About Using Relative Pronouns

要把關係代名詞和前後句子的關係一一解釋清楚，恐怕說上三天三夜也扯不清。簡單來說關係代名詞前面一定有個名詞，關係代名詞的那個子句，就是把前面不夠完整的意思，再補充說明一下。舉例來說：

John works for a company.
約翰在一家公司上班。

嗯…非常平淡的句子，到底是怎麼樣的公司呢？

John works for a company <u>that</u> makes military robots.
約翰在一家製造軍隊機器人的公司上班。

哇！也太酷了吧！

看出差別了嗎？有關係代名詞和關係子句是不是讓對話豐富多了呢？其實關係子句又叫做形容詞子句，就是用一個句子形容名詞。覺得太抽象？看例子馬上就讓你秒懂：

We stayed at a <u>beautiful</u> hotel.
我們住在一間漂亮的旅館。

We stayed at the hotel <u>that you recommended.</u>
我們住在你推薦的那間旅館。

夠明顯了吧！畫線的部分都是在形容旅館，只是第一個句子用一個形容詞，第二個句子想要更仔細地說明，所以用上有主詞和動詞的句子，功能完全一模一樣，只要是問「哪個」、「哪種」，就可以用上關係代名詞和關係子句喔！

等一下！你確定已經全都會了嗎？魔鬼藏在細節裡，半瓶水響叮噹是最要不得的事，既然要學就一次搞懂吧。先問問自己，下面這些容易犯的錯誤是不是已經完全免疫了，還是依舊似懂非懂呢？

who 跟 whom 好像是通用的嘛，既然背兩個字太麻煩，乾脆只用 who 好了？

限定跟非限定用法，這些國中就學過的東西到底是什麼意思？

who 跟前面的逗點大喊不能沒有你，逗點真有那麼重要嗎？

什麼情況下，關係代名詞也可以省略？

介系詞已經夠難了，被搬到關係代名詞

前面又是怎麼回事？

除了基本的 who、whom、which、that，關代竟然還有 whose、when、where，到底有完沒完！

為什麼你要放棄治療？分析句子也有 SOP ！

天啊！那麼多東西要記，是不是心裡曾閃過搞不懂就算了的念頭呢？別急別急，只要抓著幾個要點，句子很快就會抽絲剝繭，真相大白！

以這個句子為例：

The man who is standing over there is my cousin.

乍看之下句子有兩個動詞好像很怪，但只要先將句子分成主句和子句：

主句：The man is my cousin.

那個男人是我表哥。

判斷一下，中間的子句是不是有主詞，這裡沒有，所以 who 就是代替主詞：

子句：The man is sitting over there.

那個男人站在那邊。

最後把句子組在一起：

翻譯：站在那邊的男人是我表哥。

最後如果再研究一下，原本句子中的關係代名詞是主詞，後面又有 be 動詞，可以再把主詞跟 be 動詞省略精簡成：

The man standing over there is my cousin.

是不是很 easy 勒！以後看到每個句子，只要試著分解，就會比較容易懂喔！

# 那個正在和朗恩交談的女生是他姊姊。

▶ 所有的情況都可用 that 當關係代名詞嗎？

你先選選看

A: You won't be free this weekend?
B: No. My youngest sister, **who / that** lives in Boston, is coming to visit.

A: 你這週末沒空啊？
B: 沒空。我住在波士頓的妹妹要來看我。

Ans: who

A: Which brother is Michael?
B: He's the one **who / that** works as a lawyer.

A: 兄弟裡哪個才是麥可？
B: 他是當律師的那個。

Ans: who / that

▶ that 通常可以代替關係代名詞 who、whom。

The girl who Ron's talking to is his sister.
The girl that Ron's talking to is his sister.
那個與朗恩正在交談的女生是他的姊姊。

▶ 但用來表示對象只有一個的「非限定用法」時，也就是關係代名詞前方有逗點的狀況下，who 並不能用 that 來代替。

The new teacher, who started teaching this semester, is very strict.
這個學期開始任教的那位新老師非常嚴格。

# 致相關人等：

▶ 當關代為人時，用 who 和 whom 的差別為何？

🔍 你先選選看

A: How should I start the letter?
B: How about "To **who / whom** it may concern:" ?

A: 我這封信的開頭要怎麼寫？
B: 寫「致相關人等：」如何？

A: Which Patrick are you talking about?
B: The Patrick **who / whom** was in our French class last semester.

A: 你說的是哪個派翠克啊？
B: 就是上學期我們法文班上的那個派翠克。

Ans: whom. who

▶ whom 專門用作受格關代，然而句中的關代到底屬於「主格」還是「受格」，有時候很難分辨，因此可以將句子先拆成兩句去判斷：

The teacher died last month. You like that teacher best.
那位老師上個月過世了。你最喜歡那位老師。

→The teacher <u>whom</u> you liked best died last month.
你最喜歡的那個老師上個月過世了。

▶ 這裡的關代是用來指稱 the teacher，由第二句看來，老師是受格，接受 like 這個動作，因此關代要用 whom，不過通常在演講或正式寫作比較不常用 who，口語中都還是用 who 居多，並沒有那麼嚴格的分別。

HAPPY NATIONAL DAY

{ **十月十號是我們的國慶日。** }

什麼時候關代 which 前面要加介系詞？

🔍 你先選選看

A: Which room was the victim murdered in?
B: That's the bedroom **which / in which** he was murdered.

A: 那名受害者是在哪個房間被殺害的？
B: 那間臥室就是他被殺害的地方。

---

A: When is your country's national day?
B: October 10th is the date **on which / which** our national day is celebrated.

A: 你們的國慶日是什麼時候？
B: 十月十號是我們的國慶日。

Ans: in which, on which

▶ 通常 which 作為指稱地點的關代，前面會加上介系詞，等於 where；若 which 當關代用來指稱時間，前面也會加上介系詞，就等於 when：

This is the place <u>where</u> the peace treaty was signed.

= This is the place <u>(that)</u> the peace treaty was signed at.

= This is the place <u>at which</u> the peace treaty was signed.
這裡就是和平條約簽訂的地方。

💬 都幫你整理好，不要再問了！
which 作為指稱「地點」或「時間」的關代時，
介系詞 + which 即等於 where 或 when。

214

{ 那個紅髮女孩是誰？

▶ 關代為「人」時，什麼時機用 who？什麼時機用 whose？ }

🔍你先選選看

A: **Who's / Whose** the girl with the red hair?
B: Her name is Heather. She's Karen's friend.

A: 那個紅髮女孩是誰？
B: 她叫海瑟。是凱倫的朋友。

---

A: Is that the guy **who's / whose** wife left him?
B: Yeah. She's asking him for a divorce.

A: 那就是那個被老婆拋棄的人嗎？
B: 沒錯。她老婆要求他離婚的。

Ans: Who's, whose

▶ 第一題很簡單，是在考你 who's 和 whose 的差別，who's 就是 who is 的縮寫。這是個單純的問句，問那個女孩是誰，因此選 who's。

Who's the actor that plays Spiderman?
那位演蜘蛛人的演員是誰？

▶ whose 是所有格代名詞，後面接所有物或人（可為單或複數）：

I know the man. His house burned down.

→ I know the man whose house burned down.
我認識那個房子燒掉的男人。

# 關係代名詞總複習

請選出適當的選項（答案可能不止一個）

1. I waited for him _____ midnight, but he never came.
   A. after
   B. unless
   C. until
   D. over

2. _____ socks are those lying on the floor?
   A. Who's
   B. Whose
   C. That's
   D. These

3. Is that the guy _____ won the singing competition?
   A. those
   B. what
   C. whom
   D. who

4. I won't forgive you _____ you apologize.
   A. although
   B. even
   C. until
   D. unless

5. He started his e-mail with "To _____ it may concern."
   A. whom
   B. who
   C. someone
   D. anyone

6. Is George the one _____ forgot to lock the door?

    A. which

    B. that

    C. who

    D. has

7. I didn't remember the show was on last night _____ it was too late.

    A. while

    B. after

    C. until

    D. unless

8. The video camera lets you see _____ at the door.

    A. who's

    B. whose

    C. who

    D. people's

9. Just wait here _____ I get back.

    A. while

    B. till

    C. unless

    D. for

10. Professor Smith, _____ teaches history, is my uncle.

    A. whom

    B. someone

    C. that

    D. who

解答

1. C    2. B    3. D    4. C, D    5. A

6. B, C    7. C    8. A    9. B    10. D

國家圖書館出版品預行編目 (CIP) 資料

惱人啊！講 N 遍你還錯的英文文法：EZ TALK 英文問題集 /
EZ 叢書館編輯部作 . -- 初版 . -- 臺北市：日月文化，2014.12
224 面；17X23 公分
ISBN 978-986-248-423-4
1. 英語　2. 語法
805.16　　　　　　　　　　　　　　　　103018770

**EZ 叢書館**

# 惱人啊！講N遍你還錯的英文文法：EZ TALK 英文問題集

作　　者：EZ TALK 編輯部
編　　審：Judd Piggott
筆　　者：Judd Piggott、Mandy Wei
責任編輯：韋孟岑
特約編輯：陳彥廷
封面設計：Enya
版型設計：Enya
內頁排版：建呈電腦排版股份有限公司

發 行 人：洪祺祥
第二編輯部
總編輯顧問：陳思容
第二編輯部
副總編輯：顏秀竹、葉瑋玲
法律顧問：建大法律事務所
財務顧問：高威會計事務所

出　　版：日月文化集團─日月文化出版股份有限公司
製　　作：EZ 叢書館 / EZ TALK
地　　址：台北市大安區信義路三段 151 號 8 樓
電　　話：(02) 2708-5509
傳　　真：(02) 2708-6157
電　　話：(02) 2917-8022
傳　　真：(02) 2915-7212
網　　址：www.ezbooks.com.tw
客服信箱：service@heliopolis.com.tw

總 經 銷：聯合發行股份有限公司
印　　刷：中原造像股份有限公司
初　　版：2014 年12 月
定　　價：300元
I S B N：978-986-248-423-4

# 讀者基本資料

■姓名 _____ 性別 □男　□女

■生日　民國 _____年 _____月 _____日

■地址　□□□-□□（請務必填寫郵遞區號）

_____

■聯絡電話（日）_____

　　　　（夜）_____

　　　　（手機）_____

■E-mail _____
　　　　　　　（請務必填寫E-mail，讓我們為您提供VIP服務）

■職業
　　□學生　□服務業　□傳媒業　□資訊業　□自由業　□軍公教　□出版業
　　□商業　□補教業　□其他

■教育程度
　　□國中及以下　□高中　□高職　□專科　□大學　□研究所以上

■您從何種通路購得本書？
　　□一般書店　□量販店　□網路書店　□書展　□郵局劃撥

## 您對本書的建議……

請傳真至 *02-2708-6157* 或投郵筒寄回，感謝你的配合！

# 日月文化出版股份有限公司
### 10658 台北市大安區信義路三段151號8樓

**日月文化集團之友 • 長期獨享購書 79 折**

（ 折扣後單筆購書金額未滿 500 元須加付郵資 60 元） 並享有各項專屬活動及特殊優惠！

## 成為日月文化之友的兩個方法

• 完整填寫書後的讀友回函卡 傳真至 02-2708-6157 或郵寄（ 免付郵資） 至日月文化集團讀者服務部收。

• 登入日月文化網路書店 www.ezbooks.com.tw 完成加入會員

## 直接購書的方法

郵局劃撥帳號：19716071 戶名：日月文化出版股份有限公司

（請於劃撥單通訊欄註明姓名、地址、聯絡電話、電子信箱、購買明細即可）

請以膠帶封口

OH!はいぉ～ Anにょん하세Iyo! How알ゆ～

Touch the world,
It's so EZ.

OH!はいㅛ~ Anにょん하세Ilyo! How알ゆ~

Touch the world,
It's so EZ.